The Invention of Dying

The Invention of Dying

Brooke Biaz

Parlor Press
Anderson, South Carolina
www.parlorpress.com

Parlor Press LLC, Anderson, South Carolina, USA

S A N: 2 5 4 - 8 8 7 9

Library of Congress Cataloging-in-Publication Data on File

Cover image by By David Marcu. From Unsplash. Used by
  permission.
Cover design by Lea Anna Cardwell.
Printed on acid-free paper.

1 2 3 4 5
First Edition

Parlor Press, LLC is an independent publisher of scholarly
and trade titles in print and multimedia formats. This book is
available in paper and digital formats from Parlor Press on the
World Wide Web at http://www.parlorpress.com or through
online and brick-and-mortar bookstores. For submission
information or to find out about Parlor Press publications,
write to Parlor Press, 3015 Brackenberry Drive, Anderson,
SC 29621, or e-mail editor@parlorpress.com.

To the Faculty and Staff of the Institute for the Medical Humanities, University of Texas Medical Branch, Galveston, Texas

Contents

Figure 1.

"I will prevent disease whenever I can, for prevention is preferable to cure."

—*Modern Hippocratic Oath*

Nunc scio quid sit Amor

—*Virgil*

Acknowledgments to the Deceased

I would like to thank the following dead persons for their insurgence, their altitude, and their peace:

Quinton Frankton JJS
Betty Lynn Linton, Communion Islands Community
    Hospital
Dr Al Sharlton, Oleanna Paediatric Center, Philadelphia
Professor Wendy Willeran NSTG
Frankston Haran
Sylvia Umperan CINN DDS
Will T. Esveri
Dr Thaxton Hight, of the Finton Memorial Hospital, Essex,
    England
Wilfred Molle LicAc
Professor Faust C. Nannacan
Lois M. Bytels R.N.
Hippocrates
Tom Arnold PXA, National Eye Hospital, Dublin, Ireland
Dr Graham Fericirini ME FGTT OS RT
Professor Theresa Mathers RCOH
Philip Thandercaul ACO
Albert "Bert" Morrison
Dr Neville Schwartz, the Connecticut Health Center at
    Merritt
David Yonkers PSP, Akarana Rex Hospice, Auckland, New
    Zealand
Dr Rex "Ranny" Rannicorn MD

Zhang Zhongjing
Sunnabaran Rhouli, Panapoon Hat Company
Ivan Coyle Rudd
Ursula Wanzt CINI, Communions Islands Community Hospital
Samuel S__, Clerk, Communion Islands Government Offices
Laveatia Trelp, Communion Islands Community Hospital
Dr Eddie Simpson NSD

All the characters living and dying in this novel are from The
Communion Islands. I celebrate their contributions, and equally release them from responsibility for anything portrayed in
the following work. To the members of The Communion Islands medical profession who made this possible: I salute you!

The Invention of Dying

Our Story

Sleep widow'd eyes, and cease so fierce lamenting;
Sleep grieved heart, and now a little reset thee:
Sleep sighing words, stop all your discontenting;
Sleep beaten breast; no blows shall now molest thee:
Sleep happy lips; in mutuall kisses nest ye:
Sleep weary Muse, and do not disease her:
Fancie, do thou with dreams and his sweet presence-
  please her.

—P. Fletcher
*The Purple Island, Or The Isle of Man Together with Piscatorie
Eclogs and other Poeticall Miscellanies, 1633.*

1a. The Facts About Dying

Almost all so-called "facts" here are made up, human algorithms enhanced by our shared, communal fantasies, buzzards searching for pieces of our beliefs to strip off the bones of real truth. It's as if we have created these islands to embrace the metaphor of human life but have never viewed the rolling plain of that life itself, spread out as it is in front of us. This is the medical truth:

Death came to The Communion Islands in search of bats, not to interrupt our human lives, not to disrupt our general well-being. She was a woman looking for flying foxes. Fruit bats! A fruit bat lover, an amateur chiroptologist (a bat scientist, that is), an avid explorer (if exploring is seeking out that which you cannot yet understand), Death sailed from Europe in a cloche hat.

Old woman Death sailed from England. Southampton in sunny Hampshire, speaking geographically. Her deadly heritage was French and Scottish, mostly; with a touch of that darker Anglo-Saxon that frequently reaches out from the Celtic nations, and some remnants of what we call here our B.O.I heritage (Born On the Island). Something she had born in her because of her islander mother, long past. Death, let it be known from the outset, sometimes comes from within.

Death came to us to provide something of a rebuke to her European past, and a declaration (though she didn't realise it) of her erstwhile islander future. Her mother's own life—of which she knew almost nothing, because her mother, following the Fate of many islanders in her mother's day, was barely

13 when she was taken as a dark smooth native to a dank day in a cloudy London—almost certainly spurred her on.

Of course, people write these histories all the time!

I could probably write a pretty decent one of Death, make her a man most likely, and younger, swap her cloche, her beaver, her surgical bonnets for a dark green Homburg, give her a name like Ramsbottom or Finlayson-Smyth or maybe Philips-Einstein, if not for the obvious scientific connotation. Point her neat beard to match her tall black pompadour, and present her in an old plaid coat, provide her with a silly monocle and a regular left-footed gimp, as surely she must have.

But you don't want to read a pretend history of Death. Why should you? You want the real thing, so that's what I'll give you. Long live the Queen! Long Live Poetry! Long Live Independent Music!

Let's call Death what she was: a traveller, a gambler, an occasional flimflam woman and, like all true fanatics, quite possibly the saviour of us all.

1b. 1971: Dying and Love Go Hand in Hand

1.

Enter our capital today. Turn to the right. *Look there!* The streets here in Panapoon are named after famous local orchards. Little Wyntonville, Merry Pines, Golden Acres, The Apple of Your Eye. A nice little collection of basket cases. Apples, peaches, pears, apricots, plums. Great orchards once graced this mid-coast and kept us coasting coasters in a good penny. Suffice it, we're not entirely the offspring of stone fruits but stones sure do loom large in our history; along with the cored memories of ancestors with secretive fleshy tastes. *Apropos*: we once hosted the Annual World Rubber Footwear Manufacturers Convention, in the days when boots made a man and stamping through a berry patch barefoot was everybody's business. Look carefully, and you can still detect the ridged rubber footprints in our modern primordial mud here. And smell the fruits.

After one hundred, maybe one hundred and five yards, turn right again. Ignore that compulsion to swerve toward the glaring golden spotlights of *Beninni's Open Door Grill*.

"Fresh Fish Daily. Come in! Come in!"

Given all that hoo-hah, the compulsion is understandable.

"Shrimp-U-Like".

Sheesh!

"Rock lobsters!"

Rocking, huh?

Ignore this culinary aberration (place it, perhaps, in that barrel known as "Fools and The Sea"), and continue on through our capital. Here you will see her. She's entering now, one deadly step at a time, a careful clipping to her rigid boots on the old milk jetty, a ruffle of sea breeze in her dark hair, her deep blue coat collar inadvertently upturned to point to her red cloche hat. You'll be getting the drift.

"Hello. Hello. . . ."

2.

"Hello, hello!"

I suppose I have to admit right at the outset that Death entered our town on my back. It was she and I. I and Death. We two, together, from the start. She - that English doctor, that is - had been pursuing her batty hobby, by heading back to the land of her lost mother's birth. I had been piloting a small seaplane, and still do, among my other flighty faults, running supplies, scenic tours, emergencies, and so forth.

The not often quiet old woman (I soon found out) had recently emerged from my open door. I thus stood to be corrected.

"Hello. Hello."

"Yes," I said, stepping out onto my offside pontoon, and turning forthwith toward pompadoured Death beneath her bright, wide red hat.

"Where now?" she asked. O, had I known the full story!

"Where," I said, skirting along the fuselage with my calloused hands, casually, deep in the pockets of my fine yet drooping overalls.

"Yes," she said, clip-clop, a wild curl of a deep black eyebrow pointing provocatively in my direction. Death's small but sculptured head turned redly left and then redly right.

"Where should I go now . . . to find . . . him?"

"Him?" I asked, referring to our young island clerk who, as it turned out, was destined to become our first dying man. "Ummmmmmmmmmmmm."

(For reasons connected with decorum of the deceased, the rites of passage, that kind of thing, I should refrain from recording mere civilities, but I place this "ummmmmmmmm-mmmmmmm" here for all you sensitive living readers. Bless you. Suffice it, I have learned a survival trick or two from my mountain dwelling parents. But a destination for Death I knew nothing about)

"Ummmmmmmmmmmmmmm."

And, sensitively, further:

"Errrrrrrrrrrrrrrrrrrrrrrrrrrrrrrr."

That morning, I had flown up to Monkthornton. Flown, that is, on an instruction from a local crook who runs a small parcel service here, in and out of the islands and, in between selling beds to the bedridden and mitts to the mittened, sends some work my way (funnelling the frozen expressions of our irregular island visitors, who he has fleeced. I never ask what it is I carry in those boxes of his, who these people are, or why he chooses me to carry them. I consider his crookery a gift horse. Immoral as this might seem).

I picked up the passenger (namely red-hatted Death) who was waiting at the crookery, losing the blouse off her back, radioed back to the office, and flew southward, avoiding the Ackeronites, as it turned out that a storm had come in (those mountains are subject to climatic inconsistencies, just to spite me, I swear) and I wanted to avoid upturning my morient madam.

As it turned out, despite her unique credentials, Death had not come in search of victims. She was not on official business at all. She told me her plans on the way:

"The fruit bat, mister. That's why I'm here."

Death was a woman of few but loud words, and even fewer but silent limitations (we later discovered). But bats were flying there in her pompadoured belfry, perhaps obviously you could say, and in that deep hidden cave of her impossibly bleak heart too, as it happens.

"Family Pteropodidae, sub-family Nyctinmeninae," she said, peering down from my plane as we pitched and yawed over the jungle around Burdekin. "You have some of the finest specimens in the world here in these islands."

"News to me," I replied, holding things firm in a prevailing up-current, Death in the seat beside me.

"Pygmies, barebacks, blossoms, giants, speckled, monkey-faced," she said, reeling off sub-species like she was stringing out tickertape from beneath her blood red hat.

"Oh," I said, and thought for a moment, in the way that you do, that the shadows in the clouds had become winged, their souls black, their pointed fangs alarmingly close to my fuselage.

"You'd be surprised," she continued, staring downward but her words floating upward. 'Do you know . . . ?' Face still facing beyond the plane. '. . . a fruit bat can carry the most deadly of all diseases but never, never ever mind you, suffer from that disease?'

"I did not know that," I said, genuinely impressed. Old Death, you'll be pleased to hear, knew her stuff.

She flashed a set of dangerous teeth at me so even but so contrasting in color, one against another, that she appeared to have swallowed a piano.

"Entirely true," she said.

Subsequently arriving before I had predicted - "We'll be there by 5.00 pm, Doc." it was barely past 4.30. I landed with a jolly "Whippy!" and a thin curl of my brute lips.

So what now?

"Go?" I said, no doubt looking quizzical as I jumped to the jetty.

"Sure," said the Death, "sure", taking hold of her black case I began unloading at her from the stowage hole beneath the aft pitot plate, a case that I had placed there a little over two hours before.

"He? You said . . ."

"I said?" I asked.

I said many things in my daily attention to my duties among tourists, some more beautinious, than others, I dare admit, but I didn't recall the mention of our (soon to be dying) clerk. Deceased of the Communion Islands governmental offices, as he was to be; descended in his early teens to the islands' coastal rim, as many of us did, and now was stuck there like a young shellfish on the rim of the coast. I didn't recall mentioning him. Not at all.

So be it! Circumstances dictate, I have long found, that the cockpit of small plane is no place to fence with ideas, and certainly not with Death. Experience shows, tools in hand, that you are better off capping ideas in a cockpit with a slim reference to a recently visited relative ("Dear ol' Nancy, oh dear, oh dear, oh dear"), or turning a determined ideaist to the West with a note on your brawny religious beliefs. My favourite, though, is to conjure up my personal interest in certain breeds of cat. "The Burmese has its cute ways. Now, let me tell you a thing or two." And: "Do you know the ordinary story of how the ordinary tabby got its ordinary name?" *Meooow.*

Though our young clerk had already turned his hands to many things in his time on the flatlands, he had never met Death.

"Along the front," I said, looking at the squat dark bat-loving old deceaser, whose red hat was now in her hands. Adlibbing. Pointing. "Third wooden building on the left." Or thereabouts.

And so, black case rampant, Death's pompadour went winging its way down the street.

Or so I thought.

3.

Apropos Death.

Why would a smart woman devote herself to demise? I mean, what's in it for her? Some say there is wealth. But that is a misnomer. There is no wealth in true, honest dying. It is entirely devoid of gain. Years pass. In another vein, there is always income forthcoming for a general physician, for a specialist surgeon, for a renowned pulmonologist, for a fine thorapologist, for a companethesist. But Death moves through education to training and nothing pertains.

Already she smells like the pungent inner lips of a dark blue jar of Vaseline. Poor Death! She walks with a short, tottering gait, brought about by her long determined hours "at the table". She sleeps in conversations and wakes in the middle of dreams. And she speaks hardly at all, and then only in riddles. Ask her a direct question and she replies in inanimate chestnuts and fated aphorisms: "Time spent on your colon is time well spent." "You are the by-product of your pancreas." "Beware of the cunning trips of your feet."

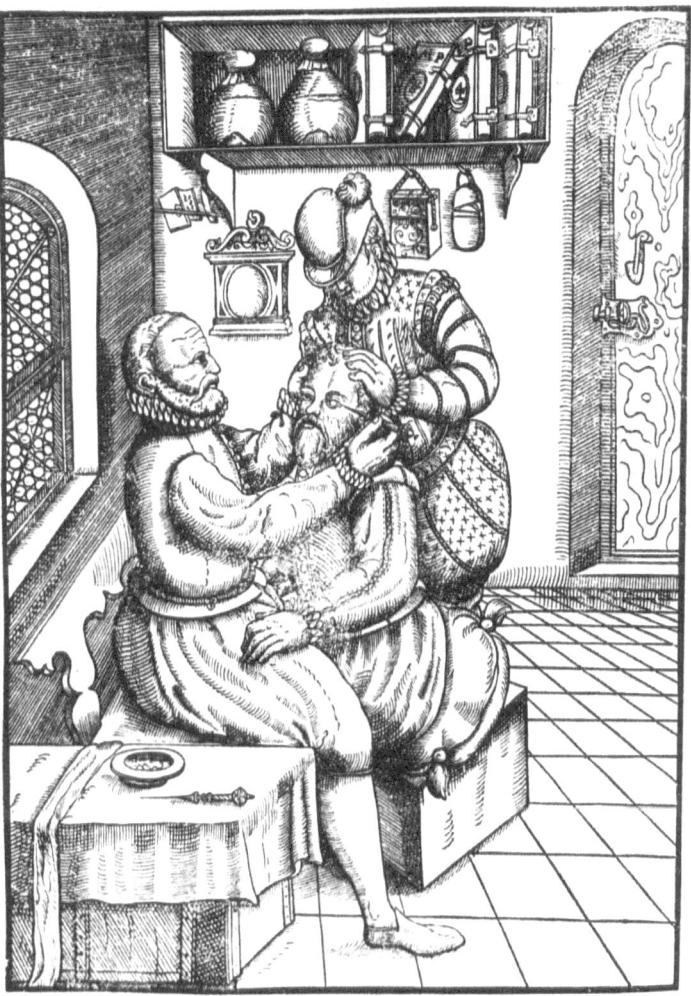

Figure 2.

There is no glamour in this madness! This is no wealth in this! No gain in this damaged cause. . . .

Incidentally, I am not denigrating manly Life, the well-known *vie de l'homme*, as he is known in those wondrous healthy health camps and the like. *Männlich leben.* In fact, manly Life was almost certainly going to be appointed the first official medical practitioner here in The Communion Islands. He was on his way to provide for us, was manly Life. But, because of a poverty of traditions of human healthcare here (you could say), and a lack of attention to detail perhaps, because he was morally flawed - because of bat loving Death arriving ahead of him, circumstances changed. Who knows what would have happened if I hadn't flown her in!

But thus, if not devoting yourself to mortality in the name of wealth, then why? For fame?

Ha! *Ha, ha!* How much of Death do you know? Truly? How many times have you been intimately acquainted with her? Poured her coffee over breakfast? (Caffeine thins the blood!) Shared some home-bake? Watch that cholesterol! How many times does Death reach the heights of even minor celebrity? Perhaps in those occasional TV appearances when you see her "on" in cafes and bars on the beachfront or in the lobbies of larger hotels, spread-eagle on the floral floor or crashing through a fish tank? But no, perhaps not even then. Death can visit a department store unguarded, and stand in a long line unattended, even as she arrives at her very moment. Death can drive through small towns at speed, without a posse of police, a signpost of sheriffs. Not Death! She can dig her front garden in broad daylight, black as the heart of good garlic, until her breath races and the sweat pours off her deceasing brow. Plant petunias even, she can, create borders of lilacs in a climate (incidentally) not conducive to either. And still no one, no one at all, notices. She takes holidays to "resorts", in sun and in shade, half-naked as the day she was . . . and is subsequently ignored around the vibrant morning buffet.

"Nice eggs, lady. What's with the scythe?"

Fame? Ha! *Not so!* The Death I know is hard pressed to get someone to notice her, even as she races to the front of the stage. So . . .

Money? Fame? No! Then it must be, you say, because Death is among us devoting herself to a higher cause. That Death (Angel of the Abyss, Pesta, Mother Time, Santa Meurte, Rider of the Pale Horse, the robed skeleton, Namuss and Lean, Woman in the Wind, The Final Encountress) is seeking out the otherworldly that dwells beneath (or beside, perhaps) the daily lives of you, or I or others we know? Death commits to the co-committant. Impossible science! *Yaahah!* She is a signatory to the cause of unsuccess! That Death (forthwith and so forth and so on) here on The Communion Islands hereby devotes herself to the inner workings of human fading so that in each unseen aspect of you and I, our loved and our loving, our superlunary selves, through the delving into the deep moment of heartache or the reasons for an unexpected lump, in seeing you before 9.00 or sending you for a test, in laboratories shiny and wet with life or in the hardbound leather of a hard to comprehend journal and the hard cold pad of a scope, in couches and on beds, in cases of glass and mahogany where dwells an unknown bone, or so it seems, and the metallic instrument of some rarely discussed human truth, in the steady gaze of concern or the conventions of knowledge so specialist that the language is another country, another planet even, Death, unafraid of the unseen or of darkness, determined, unrelenting, given to live where we ordinary folk will not, principled, pursuing, a brave soul, a braver heart, this one, ours and theirs together, being equipped and installed at our forefront, is devoted entirely, without reticence or grimace, to the cause of human departure.

Do you know this woman intimately? No? Then know this: the truth of the matter is far more complicated.

4.

"You know what?" I said to Mee (now appropriately dead), as I stepped into our breezy seaside office in the world of the living, "word is that Rudd is going out to Spook Reef tonight to hunt for the elusive razor eel."

Mee, Rudd: two living humans. An electric eel sparkingly slithered between the two of us and out onto our earthen runway, metaphorically speaking.

"That's a surprise," murmured Mee, into a nearby manila file, his thinning auburn hair aflame and his good eye alight, "I would have thought it was the wrong moon."

"Oh," I said, "You know something about The Moon? I thought you were more the terrestrial type? Earth. Larvae, wrigglers, grubbage, and the like?"

Mee shrugged hugely, like an old silver ape perplexed with an abandoned bean tin.

"Don't get me wrong," I said, "I don't doubt you've eyed the Heavens. But you're hardly a cosmologist, are you?" I said.

He seemed to be contemplating the attitude of our solitary rubber plant as it dipped its wide open arms toward the even more open window and the blistering sun beyond.

"No matter. Razor eel wait for no man."

Poor Mee. Pronounced "mere", incidentally; not, as some insist, "mea".

Meanwhile, down at what then sufficed as the local clinic bat-loving old Death had turned up and, not to put too fine a point on it, all Hell was breaking loose.

5.

"I demand to see him," she cried, having explained this three times previously, one shot fired closely across the bow of another. Math is immortal, as many will know. You might expect that these previous requests go largely unrecorded, but here is the extent of it:

I don't want to bore you with meandary. Suffice it, Death had "wished", she had "desired", and she had "wanted". With each addition to her ghostly barrage her voice rose a full octave, climbing the ladder of trouble. *Tres loon!* The bat-loving necrologist was now fully firing.

Perhaps there is something in the bat world of Death's that would explain her irritation, her lively unrest there on the harbour front. Something in the world of the dying that is batly antithetical to our more general human understanding and feelings for life. Something frugivorous or nectarivorous, that comes with gritted variegated culmination and cannot be understood until you reach this, a blindness to a lack of person, to a person's clear non-presence—because at that point Death was darting her eyes back and forth, from one corner to another of that front room of the office we locally called 'the clinic'. No foresight could confirm the lack of the county clerk, no hearing could hear him there. But maybe, just maybe, that was what was going on, as Death flapped and swooped and echolocated her deadly way around the room. Perhaps it was this thin-winged and short-tempered battiness that drove our first encounter with Death to demand from the pale young woman behind the counter more information. Perhaps it was that Death's mother had been born on the islands herself and her sense of inherited ownership flowed, much like lava seems to possess a sense of right as it engulfs your garden shed and makes its way up over the gasping family dog.

"Well, no," said Penny Apple, white haired and priming one of her well known grimaces that doubles as her youthful smile. That smile sat on her pale pink lipsticked lips like a bright fly before her withering voice, "he is not . . . here . . . yet. But. . ."

Or perhaps, speculating a moment - and this is always possible - perhaps bats had nothing to do with what was unfolding in the clerk's office, and Death's motives were far more self-serving than we were ever to discover, either then or now.

"*Buuuuut?*" Death cried, positively (and negatively) charged, all at once. An increasingly ionic pompadoured bat-lover.

"Well, mam . . . " began Penny, attempting to approach hot inveigling Fate; but then, noticing the fatefully darkening wings above front of her from across the clerk's desk, fell into such a white fuzz behind the counter of the clerk's office that she already appeared more like a shiny statue of a girl than an actual living person.

An aside: the current Communion Island Apples are, as their very name suggests, remnants of a long lived dynasty of local apple entrepreneurs ("An Apple a Day . . . ") whose orchards once began at southern Mount Welson and, travelling the lower slopes as the best apples do (on account of the frost and the weeviling life that dwells beneath those rocky overhangs), spread down around Routville and Morphew, along the thin winding road that links Haymon and Casemont and Toobay, until they come to rest in silvery sheds and a striped bun-tinged stall on the outskirts of Panapoon.

"Mam," the girl attempted again, apple of her cheeks now so brightly polished as to reflect the visitor.

At that moment, as if somehow Apple ancestors were watching and chose to step in before tall, thin Penny (carved something like the stick on which a candied red delicious might sit; bleached of color and teetering there in full white mane) grew so indistinct that no one could tell her from a badly taken photograph of an opossum. At that moment, the clerk, who was no more knowledgeable then about Death than I was, no more accustomed to dying than a fence post is accustomed to the warmth and community of a kitchen, arrived.

Voila!

Sometimes you have to admire humanity for its sheer and abundant repetition of impossibility.

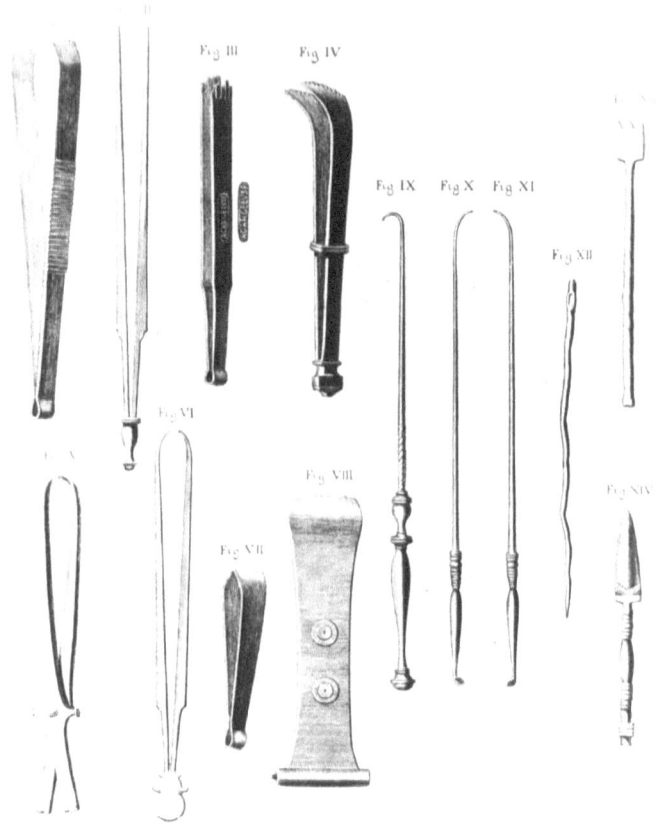

Figure 3.

6.

For those with a keen interest, and wandering ways, the history of living and life on The Communions Islands runs roughly like this:

Firstly, the islands themselves were founded in the Mycean period. By which I mean, when Communion rocks flowed over other Communion rocks in orange lit expedition, spewing from the funnel of a mountain which, mere minutes before, had been no more than a spray of something's bright intention, and nothing remotely resembling life (as we and several other planets know it, at least) existed.

This far back? Is that too far? Arguably (what does this word mean? The word is pure provocation!).

Arguably (anyway), in essence, if not for the hollow that had been created then, along an emerging gorge (aflame still, as it was), so that where, later, water began to flow in rains that came—and for some decades would not stop, incidentally—if not for that gorge then no channel would have been formed. And if not for the channel then, as the coast shifted (as shifted it did; one minute a spit of sand in the shape of a knife, and the next minute a rocky escarpment resembling the future faces of our Founding Fathers) and redefined itself, then no hummock of rich earth would have formed. And, if not for that hummock of rich earth which, as hummocks go about their business, formed and extended itself and grew and extended itself further until what was a hummock became a coastal plain, if not for this then no alluvial tale could be told. Alluviality! Richness growing on richness. Hummock upon hummock. So that by the time the Mycean period had passed to the Ferotrophic and the Ferotrophic into the Anthrohalycon—or maybe this is my invention and this particular period is largely made up.

But what the hoot! If the period fits enter it! So the first microbic flicker of our future had begun to appear, raising its microscopic head, flicking its microscopic tail, announcing its first Annual Communion Summer Fair maybe (Old Alyce Willeman's Vanilla Sponge Surprise sure seems to come from this period. *However, perhaps I digress!*). By this time, thousands of years previous evolutionarily speaking, the basics were there. The rest we can skip over. Thus:

Founding fathers, after whom future wings and wards and strolls would be named—the future *Sir* Alfred Compton Smythe, an "adventurer" (read: "mere boy, barely out of short pants", soon to be "alcoholic", sometime "swashbuckler", frequent "insomniac"), often called merely Smythe, in light of his impersonal nature; Master (of cabinetmaking, something conferred by an ancient guild) Ernst Loobenthal (known, irresponsibly, as Looby, by the locally initiated, on account of his historically irreverent nature—this being a young man who later named his sorry children Pitt, Fitt and Fortune, to exemplify some innate understanding he had of his present and his future; a man who, indeed, followed his own pioneering footsteps by making a Fortune from the Pitts he Fitted into the surrounding hills, from which he (and latterly his underlings, miners, managers, train monkeys and, not to put too fine a point on it, slaves, extracted rare minerals and malekites: rutile, ancoroar, malisinite [used in the making of typewriter keys, the controls of cookers and, in later years, the triggers of certain pistols). And, finally, Walter Winifred Breezer Esq., on which more (or definitely not more) later.

But *enough*! Distant relatives bear the substance of personal madness (I say this having no idea of what it means, but knowing exactly how it feels). Suffice it: Walt Breezer was our first town mayor, at eighteen years old he had been as bold and as firm as an iron bar—and my great great grandfather, so called. A young lively islander of infinite, unwieldy gall.

Anyway, yes, young (men, mostly), Founding island boy Fathers. A remote settlement of high living juveniles, carefree islanders of mixed race and the like. An infant settlement, as many imperial settler communities are, of course. One hundred and fifty new souls stumbling in the rich alluvial soil of the Welsonians (the far mountain to the South: South Welson; the closest mountain: Middle Welson, the far mountain to the North . . . *You get the mountainous drift!*). This was a period of uncertainty which lasted, by all estimates, several lifetimes.

Everyone, and I mean *every*one here in those early days, lived life before they even knew it! Of course, there followed the great plague years which scarred but did not ultimately kill our population. You can see that on Water Street which runs (no pun intended) alongside the main beach and looks not unlike a puzzle, one (now worn) brick angularly placed against another, one line lined up against another, like a series of coded possibilities without a code, so that as you look along Water it does indeed appear as unfathomable as water, points where the lines of its bricks seem to flow fast together and other points where they seem tangled and stagnant, points of clear bright colour and other points of dark cold, and all with the intrusions of the remnant bleached posts of jetties from which the ill were transported in ships to countries way beyond the Communions, and never seen again.

All this is recorded in the most well-known local history books *The Communions Islands: the First 150 Years* [1962], by T. K. Algebrine, *Our Beloved Communions* [1964], by the Rev. Horace C. Precious and, though often ignored, the long and complicated history entitled *The Trouble with The Communion Islands* [1973] by Walt W. Breezer. Yes, him) because it seemed that those who did not leave, who survived all things in their homes, their half-build shacks, their half-built fishing boats, survived, survived and, subsequently, survived some more. Alternatively, those who were taken away never came back. The ships returned empty. So it is from there, from those beginnings, where youth persisted, and from that The Communion Islands were made. We were a population still learning the alphabet of life. We had no place in it for Death.

"An Island of Children!" disingenuous headlines from other, close-by islands declared.

"Child's Play on the Communion Islands" went others, which a hint of envy, I thought.

"Paedi At Tricks!"

But those envious declarations were beside the point because, once inaugurated as a nation, The Communion Islands entirely made its own way in life.

Until, that is, the arrival of Death.

You can see that early period in the island fishing families, young but with an ocean heritage of "near-Death" experiences (near-Death is a strange term, because they were nowhere near her at all, actually; but, so they assumed when one of their fishing boats sank or a black shark took a hunk from a tuna as they hauled it in); the youthful timber-getting families whose members fell under a falling cocoplum tree but rose again soon after, like saplings; the adolescent orchardists struck by lightning but only singed; the half-grown miners, dusty in search of precious stones, communities and opals and the like, and suddenly clasped by the earth in stones, only to have them crawl out from their collapsed tunnels into the sunlight.

The Communion Islands were raw and so distant, connected by a coral outcrop to each other, and several named but unrenowned seas. And yet living sometimes came with a price. The way an eye of a Communion Islands child appeared, for example, sometimes to have no ending. Not in its shape or size or the color of its pupil. But something else, in its depth, so that as you looked into it you felt yourself slipping from your moorings, coming adrift. Falling inward, as it were.

I should know: I was one of these kids.

Children from families like the Eddins and the Drinkerds, the McOrdles and the Beards, the Yorks and the Blackspikes. It was there. The Hurleys and the Handinos, the Lakehams and the Curbows. To name just a few of the pre-deceased local dynasties. I ask: "How many of these pursued that trait of haruspex desire?" Connections, that is, with the animal kingdom of the Communion Islands. Seeking answers in the ways of creatures. "*Plenty!*" I answer. Out in the trees, or in the sea, up in the mountains, along the trails of opossum and amper deer, black parrots, and fur mice. "How many seemed to carry no other scent but the occasional scent of ether and antiseptic and gauze and benzoin?" (Home medicine sufficed! That is, you've heard the expression "Smells like Death"? Well, they never did!) How many had bones so supple that even after falls from heights—such as the crumbling clay cliffs above Skelton Beach or treed ridges of La Roneo - they continued unscathed.

To those from other islands, who came to discover these islands, the children of the Communions only seemed to become ever stronger, never weaker, only to be ever more healthy never more ill, only to be becoming ever more permanent, never less so.

Alternatively, the visitors themselves felt themselves staggering onto and off these shores. Across their brows grew furrows, furrows appearing as they observed us. Typically (if any of this could be said to be typical) two furrows, above their eyes, and some just below them. Horizontal, and lateral, like crossing train tracks (as many of these long distance travellers bore, none too happily, inscriptions of ordinary, dull, human experience clashing with what they now observed of our lies). And their particular furrows were particularly angular, riding over the cheekbones of these island visitors like the waves of our rising sea swell, up and over. And onwards. And these furrows moved too, they altered, as they discovered more about our ways of living. From initially shallow to soon deep, from light to dark, from narrow (mere lines) to wide (gullies), from short (an inch, maybe, perched over cheekbones) to long, flowing, impossible, heading into the distance, beyond. You might even say that these Communions furrows— which island visitors observed in mirrors as their time on the islands lengthened - reminded our visitors of the tearing teeth marks of something truly enormous.

But back to our history! To cut a long story short: after the Mycean-to-Anthrohalocyn periods, those half-formed primal brutes, then The Communion Islands saw more steady and more concerted growth—devoid finally of the restrictions of potential but never complete malady and disorder that infected the Founding years and borne forward, increasingly, on the fundamentals of minerals, fisheries, wood and fruit. The four pills of Life, perfectly served by The Communion Islands.

The burgeoning 21st Century burgeoned onward. *Yippeee!* Modernity. Tourism began. . . .

(See there in this, our fine cinematic vista of time, the bright green horse-drawn tour bus of the Communion Islands Private Bus Co Ltd [Thomas Seawell, proprietor], taking adventurous visitors out along Water Street, weekly, and onto the meandering miles of the Gushing Highway [highway in name but not in action; road holes so large as to accommodate towns. Gushing [the name of an island government road builder of yore] it ain't], on their way to staying overnight at the Toobay Inn, which in later years would be owned by Seawell himself, who had traipsed out there one high season toward the end of the century, taking a gaggle of eager travellers in their leather boots and white flounces, and, for reasons best known to Fate, promptly decided to stay in the room overlooking the small courtyard from which the high green peaks of South Welson can be spied but very little of Toobay Bay - thus why he took the room, to give visitors the best views of blue whales and waterbirds, and the steaming sails of the fishing fleet, in the hope they might understand us. And for this he subsequently stayed eternally without any sight whatsoever of the ocean, for which he had an almost impossible affection)

All the while, growing Communions around it, trees came down—hardwoods, softwoods, apple and orange woods, woods for train tracks, woods for homes, woods so exotic that they were sent to cities in remote provinces or given to Kings by Heads of State, woods that swirled with grainy mysteries, woody contrasts, hardened seams, softened stratums— and as these trees came down, beneath them, way beneath the alluvial coast and beneath the rising mountains behind us, beneath rich soil and once volcanic rock, men and machines burrowed for wealth.

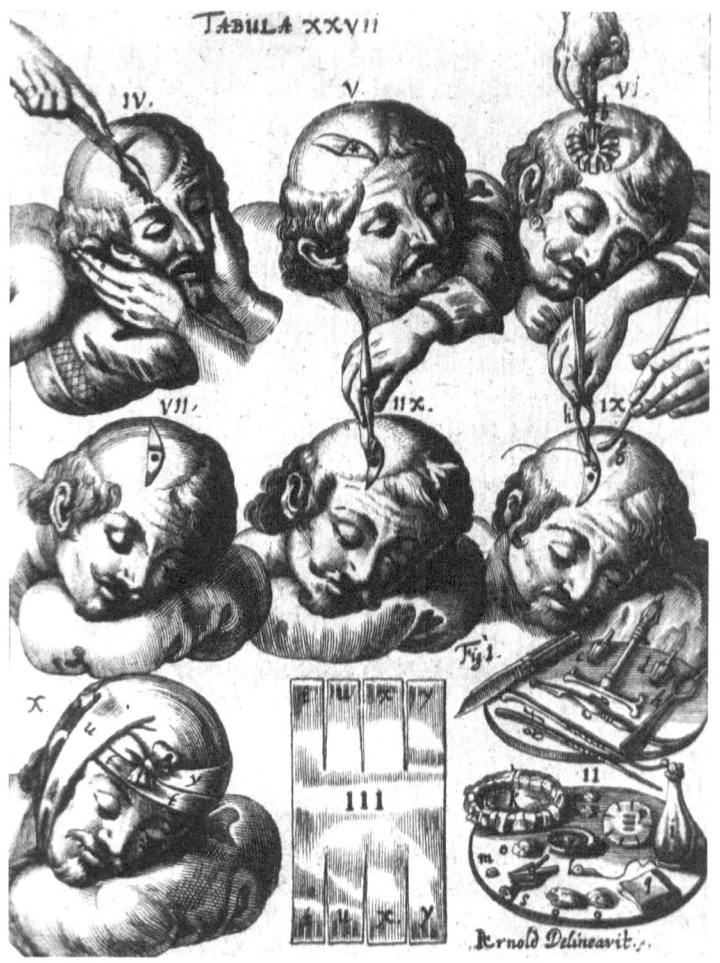

Figure 4.

7.

Suffice it to say, before the arrival of Death, danger here on The Communion Islands consisted entirely of a knife and a block of volcanic stone on which to blunt it.

Men certainly lost their way, but nothing became of it. Women became ill with half-born children and themselves alike, simultaneously, but they always recovered. Infants fell at the feet of their vibrant island parents, and were simply picked up. Life expectancy—strange concept that!—life expectancy for those who never left The Communion Islands was, simply, Eternity. We were a nation composed almost entirely of brown skinned children, tanned, tempering in the island sun, and permanent.

Consequently, we looked at our local world as abject novices, never old enough to be old. We were constantly beginnings, not more, but determinedly not less. Openings. Alphas. Originals. Island kids in all our unadulterated kiddery. Flowing with new and unfathomable life about which we had little understanding and few concerns. We opened ourselves to everything. Why wouldn't we? How couldn't we? Why shouldn't we?

You could hear our island nascence in our ordinary daily conversations, which rarely dwelt on anything but the unknown. Indeed, today a common opening on The Communion Islands remains:

"Do you know. . . ?"

As in, "Do you know, it might rain today?" addressed to someone (say your dearest friend, or a fisherman) who you might rightly suspect would know this.

More poignantly:

"Do you know, today is a good day?"

Or more tellingly perhaps, on account of these, our origins:

"Do you know what?"

"Do you know when?"

"Do you know why?"

As you can imagine, some visitors have mistaken some idiosyncrasies in our way of speaking for irony, as if the entire population of the Communions is given over to speaking in circumlocution, real meaning hidden in the thick jungle of our belief in opposites, situations presented in determined islander reverse. Other islanders, at the time, even thought of us as cruel and unprincipled. Can you believe? Accusations were frequent that we lived a kind of metaphoric life, devoid of any real feeling, perpetually young and persistently inattentive to the problems of others and of the real world.

Ha! Let me report. A youthful islands, we craved (and had long craved) what we did not yet know.

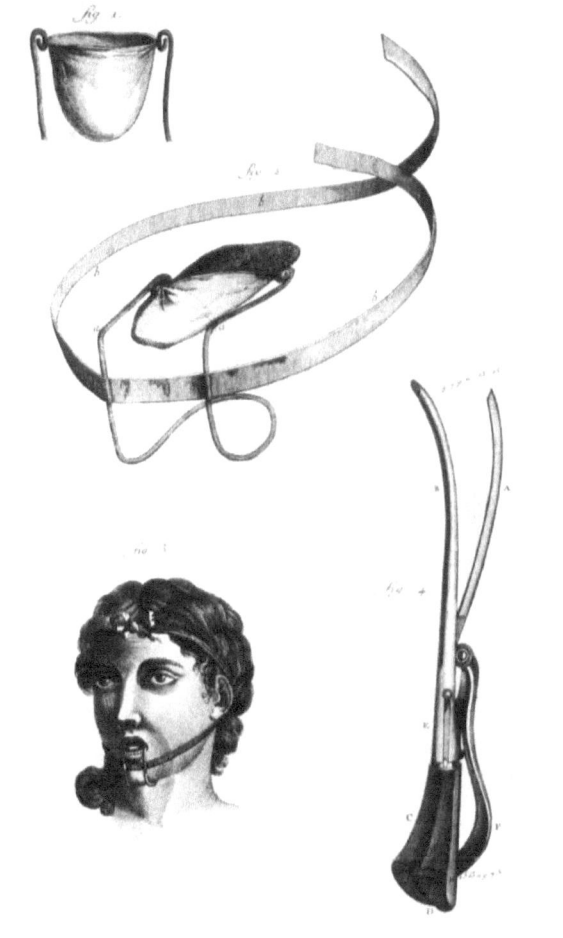

Chirurgie

Figure 5.

1c. By the Chin

And so. . .

The clerk looked at my newly delivered bat-loving passenger: Death, standing in flustered red-hatted dishevelment in front of him. Had I been a small beetle clinging to the slatted wooden wall of what was the only building in The Communion Islands masquerading as an administrative facility (scrape, scrape, scrape, I go, beetling on that Death defying wall) I'd say the two of them were propped on the frames of the two doorways, the outer and the inner, opposite. The boy, taller (but younger and less certain) and Death smaller (but weary from travel and unsure of whom she was about to address, because already Miss Apple had inadvertently failed to introduce the young man to Death, falling instead into a peculiarly satisfied grimace, as if simply observing the two of them in the same room resolved everything that had befallen her that morning).

And then, first placing her black case awkwardly down on the sandy floor, Death began, one ebbing conversational piece at a time, to draw from the young clerk the truth about The Communion Islands. And she did so by questioning him about bats.

"Have you seen any barebacks? No?"

. . .

"Blossoms?"

. . .

"Any giants?"

The young clerk entirely unaware, in return, began to tell the story of the islands, so extraordinary, so unfamiliar, and so unknown to Death that he rekindled in her something of her own barely known past and almost completely lost love of Life. He brought back in Death something she had long been missing or, more accurately, had never found.

At least, that is how we like to tell the story of their meeting.

It might have been, alternatively, that Death merely recognised a job opportunity. All that talk of an island of children and of unchartered living places, it might have been . . . All that stuff about an island of youth, and a history of self-reliance. . . All that young clerk stuff about the abundance of The Communion Islands. . . . It might have been that Death merely recognized an opportunity and, seeing it hanging there in a tree so black and yet so bright, so aware of its surroundings and yet so blind, so ready for flight and yet so surrounded by the walls of its habitat, that Death took out her enormous silver gun and promptly shot it. I know the version of the story that I prefer.

But hey, all this arrives second-hand! I merely report! No one was there but those reported: Death appearing as a bat-loving middle-aged doctor and the clerk a dark boy born in a tiny village in the Cloud Mountains. Raising their voices together, their differences more obvious than their similarities. But getting on, by all reports (though she had been around, to coin an expression, and he hadn't), as one questioned the other.

Meanwhile, pale Penny Apple, out behind the counter, began to glow so red, with embarrassment we can only assume, that she might well have combusted. The so-called "Waiting Room", now barely half full on account of it being late. Almost empty, in fact, except for the McOrdles [Mrs and Mr and their four smallest], whose children used to come down with blemishes and broken bones at the turn of each

tide; but, of course, always survive.

By the time two tales were half told Death and the young clerk were down at the Shoreline Hotel, drinking together, their voices like the barks of Fur Seals, their differences [sunny headed clerk from Upper Cuth; black pompadoured visitor , Death] thrown to the wind, until eventually they fell into slumber together on the table top, covered over only with the smiling embers of change.

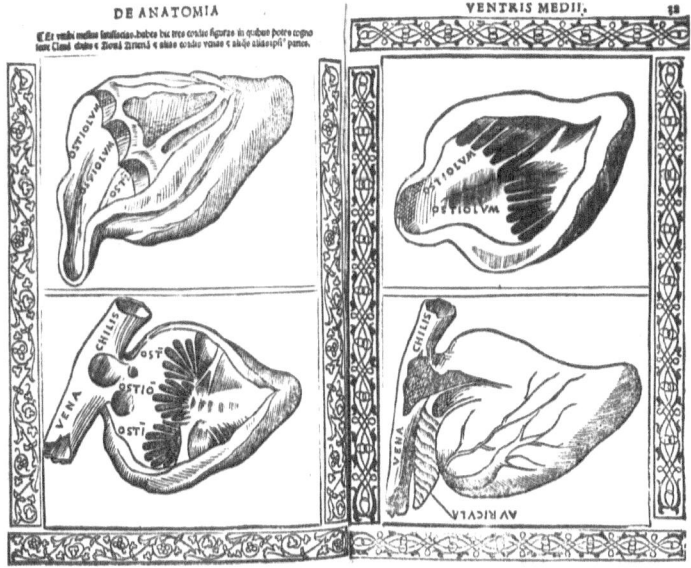

Figure 6. The Human Heart

2a. The Conception, Birth and Life of Death

Shall I insert here a long section here regarding the founding and, later, the growth of The Communion Islands? Sure, I could do that. Isn't living a lively industry?

We could spend some time talking about the building of buildings, towns and such, and then a formal section about transportation and communication, a glossary of local words with a neat historical index, a clever investigation of agriculture and pesceculture, fishing that is, a typology of island employments from sweeper to builder to butcher and baker, a nod to the arts, with a thumping local dance routine, a rollicking yarn about the power we have generated from the falling waters of streams and rivers. Perhaps for effect show the young clerk weaving himself through the scene, full of his own impending demise.

Dramatically, we could have Death flying around the islands in her shiny black cape, her memory of her own birth floating on her shiny black shoulder like a sprite of forest sunlight, perhaps a medical degree in her pocket from some prestigious school in London or Berlin or fine old Prague, to make that somber connection with her dear old ma whose body was undoubtedly preserved in a dusty glass case in a oak lined room (I make this up, but it can be imagined).

I like that idea, actually. I think if a woman comes to an island and brings about something, anything that would have otherwise not existed, something that her presence invests and inflects and bears boldly onto our island landscape, then she should be lauded for that effort.

Oh, I am a great believer in life, don't get me wrong. I celebrate the origins of people, the foundations of civilizations, the real as well as the mythological essences that thread through island undergrowth and make their way into rocks and so forth.

"Without life," I say, "where would we be?"

It's true. And, of course, Death had connections to island life, whatever else might be said of her past absence. Death, you might say, presupposed life. If I were to be philosophic about it, Death was the dedicated daughter of life.

Excuse me while I historically digress! What we had here in the islands was like living in a communal home in which was located the vast hidden foundations of the universe, among the bubbled grey mortar, that is, the strong and hefty regal red beams, the creatures that thrived on the pure earth of entirely covered human reason. It's impossible not to admire the importance of all that, as it was. It's impossible not to relate to the human importance of our living foundations. Without which . . .

There's a story told here about a wharf—what some people, in some parts of the world, apparently refer to as "a pier", and others elsewhere in the world apparently refer to as "a jetty". Strange. No matter! This wharf-pier was over on the North side of the islands near Yool Bay and Lower Yool. A Yooling jetty it was, regardless.

This was a wharf over which much timber was travelling. By which I mean, an off shoot of some famous imperial Timber Company, traders in timbers for several crusty generations, had sent in visiting teams who were working strappingly over there, bringing down from our pristine higher forests great swathes of blackwood and thropthorn, acres of brewt and those enormous philfond trunks, stripped already of their poisonous and spiky and somewhat historic branches. Those traveling timbergetters used their imported oxen in those days, not horses; and certainly not jigging trucks, whose painted, motorized growls were still some years away.

Two white sailed and foreign ships had been loading for what was said to have been almost two days. Sunburnt visiting men were moving back and forth, steering oxen teams of eighteen or twenty, up into the forest, the crack of their leather whips and the crunch of trees under wooden wheels was all you could hear. Night as well as day. That and the oxeneers' shouts:

'Whackah!"

"Fell yack!"

"Fooooowhist!"

The language of those traveling oxeneers is now a lost piece of history.

All day and all night. You can imagine the volume as mighty imperialing team upon sinewy team dragged down from our closest hills each log, the conjoined twins of blackwood, each bright bushel of brewt. Onto their ships all this was going. Along the wharf. Being lowered on ropes to the jetty.

And all would have been fine, or as fine as it might have been. Today you could probably visit courthouses in other parts of the world that are lined in the swirls of blackwood that were brought down from Upper Yool at that time. Convicted thieves in Germany, perhaps, and Sweden maybe, where crime is almost unheard of but when it is heard is monstrous (something of the northern heritage, some say), would at this very moment be hanging their condemned heads in the presence of those swirls and feeling from their radiating wisps the depth of their malfeasance.

You could go out now and purchase from an antique store in Chipping (near prim Piping and Lively Limping, in lovely outer London town, down by the parlor and the palace and other things), china cabinets of fine yellow brewt, one join melding so perfectly with another (because the brewt from that part of The Communion Islands was, indeed, the most usable brewt of all). You would barely even see where one length ended and another began. And you could still detect the aroma of camphor in the wood. You could watch as the Senate in Silesia was meeting around the government's giant philfond table and know on its sturdy legs an entire Silesian population could be held up against the flow and tempests of time and economics.

But all this is impossible, because of lack of foundation, an absence of true life. To cut a long story short, that wharf collapsed.

Those traveling timbergetters had built their structure on nothing. Nothing was sunken before it, and nothing was built on nothing to create, despite the physical appearance, absolutely nothing. That structure was little more than a bunch of sticks jabbed determinedly into our grey ocean mud. By the end of the first day it began to sway, back and forth; but those crazy sailors only took this as evidence of a rising Communions sea and simply worked faster, brought more wood to the wharf, continued on regardless.

The captains of the two ships—the Prince Leonard and the Clipper Monteroy, so called - were asleep in their mahogany cabins. It is said (By whom? Who knows!) that their plan was to sail right through the next days to deliver their loads to their faraway homes. There's a nice turn of phrase! The swaying wharf only reminded their slumbering be-hatted selves of the lolling coast around Och O Loon Reach and the outer (or is it Inner?) Hebrides, where there are no reefs and there are no calms, and the water is abundant and icily welcoming. Chances are they were dreaming, so content they must have been with their plans.

But that wharf with no life, built on nothing, had other ideas. So it collapsed. And it took those ships down with it.

First that Monteroy went down, and then that Leonard was sucked into that swirling, wet, distant, grasp. The collapsing wharf took several teams of sailors too, who had stopped on the plank walk in the early evening, no doubt to contemplate their transient work and, no longer sending their huffing steam into the night air, were soon sent plummeting toward their ultimate destination in our Communion Islands sea.

Some of those visiting ax-wielding sailors did survive, though. Back on the land. But with their ships sunk and being hundreds of tangled miles from our then small township of Panapoon, and even the tiny outposts at Store Cove and Yawl. All succumb to deprivations we today can only begin to contemplate.

We still find their bleached skeletons propped against philfonds and down beside babbling brooks, to this day. And why? Why is that? Because theirs was a modern construction built with no attention to origins, no address to the life of the Communion Islands which, not to put too fine a point on it, was all around them. Had those fine trees they were busily felling been given their voice they could have told those visitors plenty.

"Live!" they'd have said. "Life!"

And: "While we trees may not speak, we just as well could as we declare what might be, or how existence grows."

Something like that. Lord knows, I wouldn't deem to speak on their behalf.

Likewise, had the redstone cliffs of The Yool been consulted, instead of just ignored, except by the Communions

Golden Gulls that nest there and hatch their goldlings in sun kissed seagrass beds, and feed them on errant crabs and string weed and so forth, they could have reeled out enough evidence to build an entire stable metropolis. *But no!*

So what, I wonder more generally, of all the travelers and chance merchants who have made their way here to the Communions over time, the fortune hunters, the speculators, the opportunists? What is their role in our story?

If we each are not inherently evil - and my evidence suggests this has to be true: that we *homo sapiens* are good by inclination or inherited substance and it is only circumstances that . . . —suffice it then, that Death already had her assigned role too, and a no less human one, I might add.

I think of her there in my small plane seat, tall black pompadour beneath a bright green bergère hat in that case, turned toward the rattling window, her shoulders narrow and bony but undoubtedly sturdy. I hear her voice lassoing the sand around Panapoon and the slippery wet rocks of that mighty shore. I see her firm dark index finger pointing down at the Burdekin hills as I tip the plane on its aft wing and swing us slowly, elegantly, to the West, me in the sun and bat-loving Death in the shadowy dark.

I see her stride, her black case bulging abruptly, the suited men she meets, their earnest discussions, the cusp of hands, the furrowing of brows, her radar eyebrows twitching, her looks to the horizon as we stand on the edge of the runway and a tropical storm teems now over us. I think of the young clerk and his mountain dwelling family below. I think of our new town buildings being built down by the sea and up in the mountains.

I could pretend this can be captured in preliminary sketches and serious meetings: "Mining at Cuuk Town", "Establish-

ing a Tourist Center at Panapoon", "The Future of Spiny Lobsters in the Bay of Constance", "An Airstrip for Residents of
Finch Hole". The inevitable zonings and committees, the is-
suing of contracts, island developments near and far (such as
in Cloud Mountain, cloudily and Old Town, venerably, and
Cape Constable), the digging of clay, the bringing of stone,
the news stories, "Communion Islands Rise", 'Houses Built
in the Hills", "Young Future", "Healthy Here in Shelton Valley", the rising façades of our futures, the coral shell crusts for
the seafront benches, pink and black and white, the peaked
arch thropthorn doors of the rising hotels, the smoke of tree
loggers, the seafront small against the now towering cococan
marble of the Regional Council Offices, flaked gold and deep
blue as it is, the white brick, the iron gates of and, the basalt
foundation stone of a brand new elementary school.

I could describe this languid, stumbling rising of a future,
arriving day by day, week by week, month by awe-provoking
month. But I best be reminded, as others have been reminded,
that we are confronting Death.

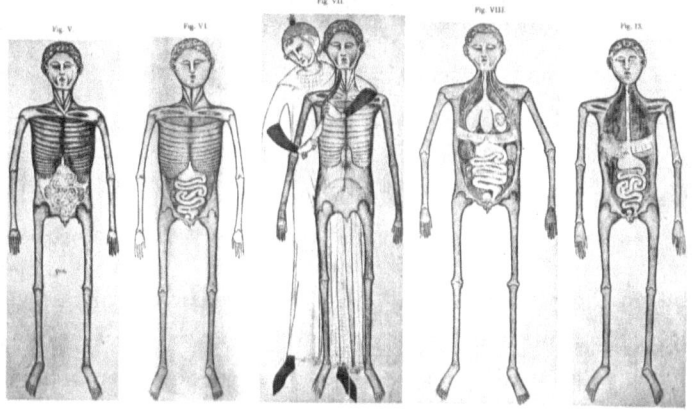

Figure 7.

2b. Certain Sounds

(named with regard to that denied human sound: *gurgling*)

Within the ears of a young clerk's family a world of futures opened up, much as a newly growing town in The Communion Islands begins to extend the boundaries out from a front door or its vibrant new future emerges from the opening of a freshly sealed window. The young clerk was, by genetic heritage, a good listener. Death would soon have her attentive audience.

Some ear researchers (I've heard!) say that there is an initial surge, like electricity, as you enter the auditory realm, and then a cusping, or clasping. Some [Drs Manning and Morton, 1971, apparently] have compared this to the effect of leaving The Earth, to the attitude of space travel: the first lift, the push through the atmosphere, the heat as you move through one layer of air after another, the moment of resistance, that almost visible steel of enclosure that arcs over progress, contains and cares, carelessly contains one substance while preventing another, the push against this, the searing push, emblating alight and now falling, in slices, spinning.

The human ear is a place, and like places it has moments, its times, its seasons, its relationship with epoch and episode. But time in the young clerk's ear was reversed, so that its duration was in the opposite aspect to our own. The reason for this, Death discovered, was simplicity itself.

As you might know, we human beings are medical complexities, our zones and operations founded on a system of impromptu performances and prestidigital balances. Observe: at one point we each appear to be in constant motion, at another as still as the granite on a hillside. When spooked, we move one way while our muscular complexions move another, like we're involved in a type of stupefied waltz. Bone, rock-like, naturally shapes us; while the lymphatic system, the system of choice and termination (I can go in, technically, for pages!), flows around this rock and down into valleys as deep as the liver and as hollow, though some do not know this, as the feet. In all this, there is infinite possibility for collapse, as one element fights against another for control (the path, as the ancients realized, for disease, detriment, death).

To prevent this, levels of performance and balance operate. "Timetables", to use a crude term. Counterweights. Organizational tools. Methods of relating, one aspect of our crazed humanscape to another, our internal personal bodification, to another; the same way the eye (for which this is a metaphor, incidentally, should you be wondering, and forms the basis of its own internal ocular world) captures the most significant aspects, and sends these for processing, while other aspects, just as seen, equally as available, are recorded in sight only slightly, sliding away behind the rest, for now at least.

So it is with us proper, our larger selves. Performances and balances. As one sets in motion, another winds down. As one holds firm another relaxes. When one escapes into its own universal existence another presents itself to our particular one. Against what we might call a singular version of time, then, in reality the human being is made of many times, multiple instants, an array of moments, counter-opposed, layered, joined or discrete.

My point is this (if I have a point, or have I made it?): were it otherwise, and something singular, we could not exist. If the *human* (so called: I must look up the origins of that word) was one time we would be no time at all. No singular instance would keep us alive and though it might appear to the uninitiated, who believe in the strength of bindery, who hold to the importance of the particular, who reject variation and complexion and association, that we are unidirectional—born and live—it soon becomes apparent, by virtue of the young clerk's hearing, by reference to them, and by understanding of the young clerk's world, his *true* and *complex* world, that singular we are not. So Death's explanation goes.

Counterpunctual. Concentrical, motioned, intersecting, additional; that, she said, was the young clerk. I paraphrase, but she said something like this (excuse my peculiar diction):

"He is like the way a centrifuge works so that as the external spinning mechanism, shiny and brass thick and bolted, is rolling over, one thick blade lumbering up over an imaginary rise, only to fall again, and then raise itself, raise itself, and then fall, fall and then . . . As this is occurring, without reason except for that which comes from continuation, within the loping rise and fall, the seeming tedium of singular purpose, another mechanism is at work. Until he reaches his proper end."

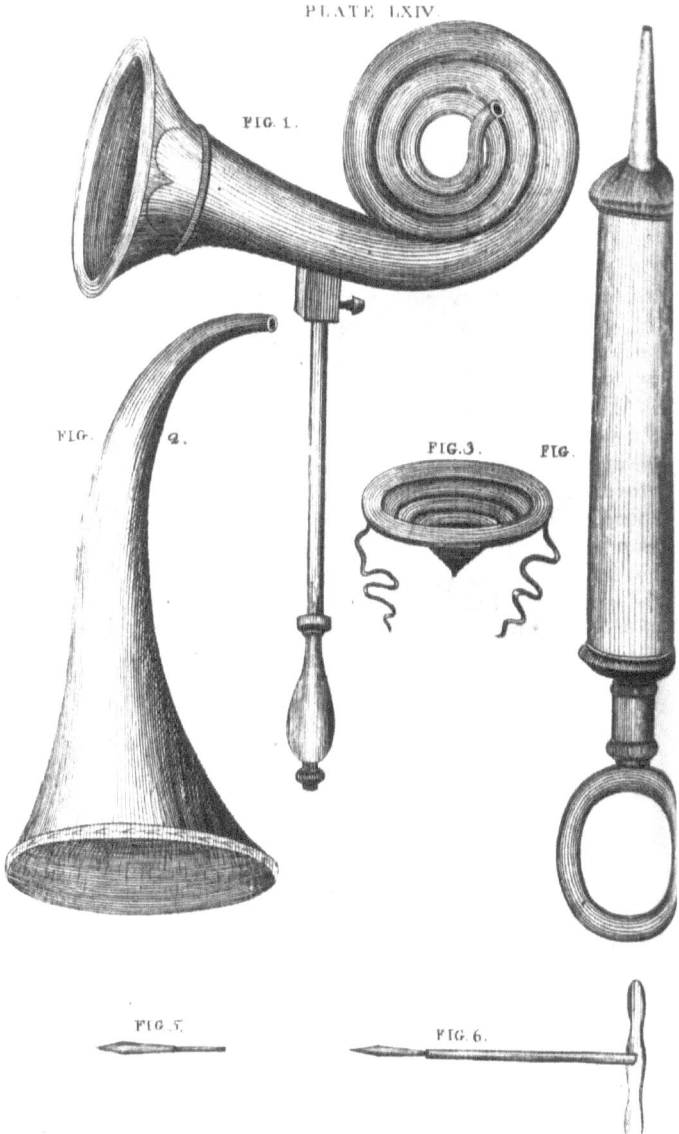

PLATE LXIV.

FIG. 1.

FIG. 2.

FIG. 3.

FIG.

FIG. 5.

FIG. 6.

Figure 8.

Waiting, 2012

1.

Here today at The Communion Islands Community Hospital a young woman (she appears much older on account of her illness, so perhaps that word of observational warning), stands unsteadily on the deep green grass again. She is staring staring *staring* out to our deep blue sea. All of the past half hour she has been teetering out there and all the half hour I have been watching her, and she me, I suspect.

In that white gown and bonnet, I suddenly imagine her to be the first bird in a gliding flock of local seagulls, as you might also perceive all the terminal patients from inside to be, the linen straps flapping behind her face, and the bay deep blue out in front of her gaze. She came down the stairs a short while ago, floating dully to the bottom, and drifted out over the wide hospital verandah with her head held up as rigid as can be and her face fixed forward.

"Can you see her?" I feel like crying out, as I imagine I know for whom, and what, she is waiting.

"Anything at all?" I call, in my head.

Death, after all, might merely send a feather of notice, or break a sunbeam to suggest a possibility.

Unlike others here now in the hospital on this hill, I don't need to adopt the physician's attending voice when I speak to the dying. I fly them in, and that's all there is to it, from remoter parts of the islands, or from near. And I know, frankly, that their real issue is curable. It is the waiting (and it's finally got too much for her, out there). But it is not necessary that I adopt the restrained curative tone of pessimistic altruism that others here adopt. I am thankfully beyond that pretense in this tropical impossible *menage* of an islands.

I've heard that in various parts of the outside world, and with due reverence apparently, The Communions Islands are referred to as "a paradise"—in ordinary conversations as well as in literature, serious travel brochures, television cooking shows and the like. Well, here's an interesting fact about paradise. Observe: there is *never* any medicine in paradise. None of the staple medical experts on survival are resident in paradise, those I have come to call our new and growing population of dedicated "ologists". Anesthesiologists, cardiologists, endocrinologists, gastroenterologists, hepatologists, microbiologists, neurologists, parasitologists, surgeons. The Communions are no paradise.

"Warm today," I say, too softly for the young woman to hear, I suspect.

My flighty role here fills me with such a sense of personal accomplishment. I'm asked to fly, collect, deliver these patients to our new and neat little hospital, and that's what I do. One minor achievement after another.

Speaking of achievement: have you ever wondered what those famous physicians from Europe thought when they discovered those bacterial cells? You know the story. Famous as fame itself, for their intelligence and their courage and so forth.

I mean, did they just up and congratulate themselves and then take off in a what? A hansome cab, or whatever? Discovering more? Or did they pause for a moment, stare at their frozen world of blown clear glass and silver steel, and think then about what their discovery might actually mean? Personally, I think they paused, just long enough to consider their new relationship with Death.

I admit, looking back to the clerk's story and its ultimate outcome, that I have probably grown the world outside The Communion Islands into dimensions that may be far larger than those that actually, truly exist. But I think too, for what it's worth, that The Communion Islands has changed because of Death and Death, though maybe she would never admit it, has changed because of The Communion Islands—become more circumspective, certainly.

"Not yet!" I call out, impulsively.

Does she hear me?

The young woman steps out onto the green grassy edge of the upper garden and by her flapping white bonnet now seems about to take off into the sky, over the cocoplum trees and yellow rocks below, to meet her end, finally, or to survey a school of silver bream, alternatively, or a scuttling gnarled brown crab.

"If anyone is visiting us today, it won't be before evening."

Does she hear me?

"The tide is out, huh?"

"Evening", mind you. Who am I to speak like this?

I've noticed lately that certain medical personnel here tend to move about their conversational languages, coming close to each one of us, moving away again. I think it calms their clinician's nerves to create colorful unfocused pictures. They seem to speak as children one minute and like some old mossy monument the next, all caught up in this play, as I might call it. I've always thought medical types know how to suggest the origins of things, the foundations of each one of us, whether they have known us previously or we've just now met. Maybe the word I am looking for is "kaleidoscopic".

Right now, as she turns slightly, I can see in her complexion the way summer has stretched its final time all about her swarthy bold forehead and onto her sweeping jaw, giving her expression a texture and what might be called a "variegation". When, what must be six or eight days ago, she came down with a fever, she didn't seem to be any brighter or bolder than she is right now—though they say that the fever causes such a delirium and a sensitivity to light that patients here can appear to be *actually* glowing, like little lamp posts lighting their small white portion of the world.

Incidentally, if on The Communion Islands we appear today to have overturned longevity, I might best clarify that we're still in entirely open conversation with the pathologies of our time (as they call them around here, medically speaking): the lagging energies, the phenomenon of creak and ache, the ominous rotting maladies, the debilitating frailties.

Her absent, invisible, life, I'm thinking, watching her, above the cove and the beach and the tripping tails of the island's green green mountains, the sight of walruses as if islands themselves, soft and silver, and fur seals shadowing the rocks around Panapoon (or so you might imagine) and the silk trees and the jacarandas. Ah, a little romance!

I wonder if any of those medical greats of Europe ever positioned themselves so blatantly in the rough so that they might club away at Death. Hear those echoes. My opinion, for what it is worth, is that that human heart is mostly a quintessence, a distillation of us, that is, rather than some kind of painted scene or a device, as it were. Medical science, huh? No, no one should have to go on waiting like this.

"*Later?*" I call out. I notice how today the sea is hardly caught by the afternoon wind, just slipping silently onto the shore as if it is some kind of luke warm child's toffee. The height of voice is impossible to determine sometimes. I could have just spoken to myself for all I know.

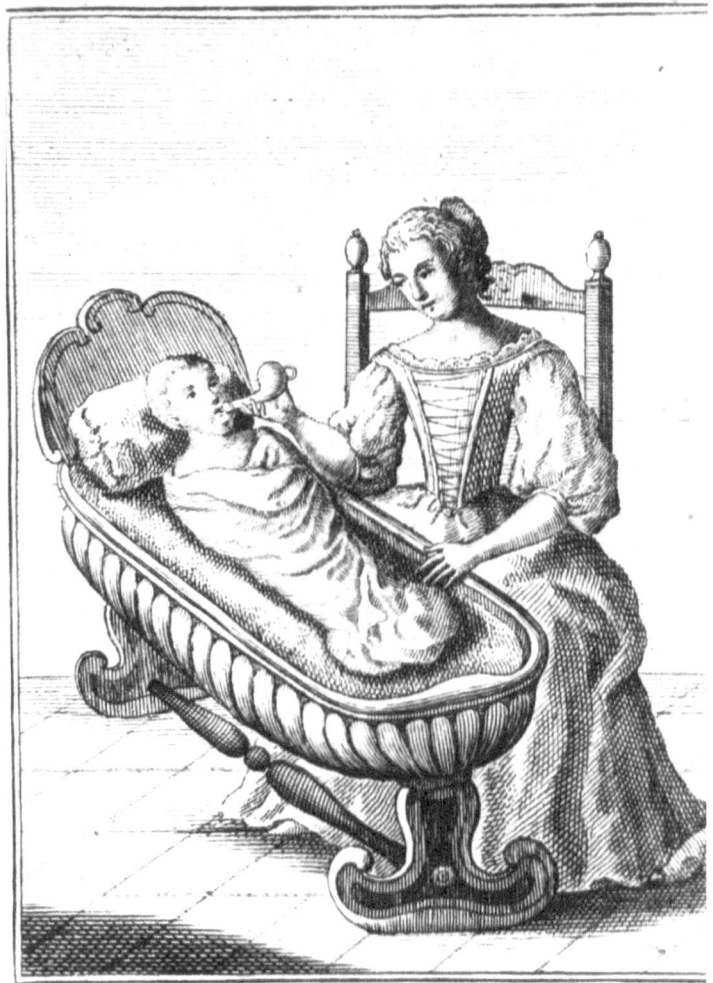

Ficta teneris immulget ubera labris.

Figure 9. Woman Feeding an Infant

Ay, if a madman could have leave
To pass a healthful day,
To tell his forehead's swoon and faint
When first began decay.

—John Keats

Our New Cemetery

1.

"What really is a cemetery?" I wonder.

"Oh," the wry might wryly say, "it is a place where the dying grow."

On evidence, who could deny such a definition? Planted, watered, tended, as they are. A garden of the dead.

You might say further, if you know a little of horticulture and feel emboldened (perhaps because you are looking out in the bright morning from your bright room in the Coral Thorn Hotel, and noticing that the amberjack are really schooling on the eastern sandbar today and the crocodile slithering along the mud banks—if that's what those shadows are), that our new island cemetery is an accommodation for growing, organized in such a way that it encourages abundance, and presents proliferation.

So, for example, you say, that this is the reason for the runnels that have been dug so diligently down from the distant hillside, not directly, but so that they travel along beneath the branches and leaves of trees and shrubs and give to the new graves the requisite "food".

Fluid, water, call it what you will. But not rain, because that (I'd perhaps boldly surmise) is your point. A properly constructed new cemetery, beside a new hospital, above a rumbling town, beyond a rising sea, deals in its own kind of organization, so though it may look to the uninitiated that these runnels are for the diffident support of rainwater running over roots, that they are dug to funnel and fudge an ordinary expectation of a flow, the truly knowledgeable of cemeteries will know that this is incorrect. Everything in the design of a cemetery works on alternate principles.

Cemetery. Cemetererian. Cemetecultural. Have you ever wondered why dealing with the dying is *not* explored as a true grand human trade and as a wondrous human set of attainments? What miraculous reasoning can this be that beyond those religious connotations, which a pagan or partly pagan islands might mostly avoid, or at best treat with song and some innocent gracing of floral tributes and closed eyes and mumbling toward the ever unresponsive sky, that the skills of dealing with the dead languish under a shoulder of silence, exist beneath the current of the daily river of happenings, neither represented nor discussed nor really displayed. Out at the new Panapoon Cemetery . . . *Hold on! Wait a minute!* Witness your necrotic tour guide:

Turn left on Water, drive fifty yards on Yeardly, turn right on Pierce, proceed. . . . one hundred, two hundred, three hundred (Pierce is a street of many underlying conditions and shapes; it was the first ever in the town and founded on the simple measures of need and circumstance. At one point a tumbledown shed made of plank and iron, at another a "box room" [so called] where the boxes were once constructed to carry freshly caught fish on hard axed ice to the towns in the north, you can tell its intention from the overhang of mighty awnings under which these fish boxes would be stacked out of the way of bad winter weather and the like; at another still the porched and balustraded mansion "Milton Park", a house once owned by Milton Peck, who was our first butcher and fish-monger [the house now owned by a wealthy yachtsman who "puts up here", I believe that's the nautical term, on his way to the Caribbean or Black Sea or somewhere, all tangled in ropes and leather-laced boat shoes. He seems to have more female companionship than a department store, and about as much concern for his surroundings as a swiftly passing arrow]; then three of the old lighthouse keepers' homes, one for each of the families and one for the bosun's mate, sturdy and dark each one, made of what we call here around here "blue stone", a kind of deep cobalt colored rock threaded with the texture of woody fur; then a modern home, brick, tall, blonde, thin and peaked with fantasy architraves, turrets and minarets, a retired couple by the name of Smallwood [possibly magicians, I figure, or a fallen high-wire act], keep to themselves, moved up from Morphew to hunt for seashells, those sneaky calci-fied Devils). By now you are almost at the end of Pierce, have pierced it, as it were! Swing, quickly, before the final rise onto the headland. Onto Marshall. And then proceed.

Now the back of town is opening up. You can see there the playing fields where many a match has been played, in time and in jest. Football, handball, loopball, loonball, you name it! And now the side road that springs out toward the garbage dump. Avoid this, for the sight and smell of this in the bright morning is nobody's business. Continue.

The road is dirt and a kind of weatherworn sandstone now. Sallow dust rises behind like so much stage mist before the emergence of the principal actor. In the summer you can disturb basking lizards and the occasional elongated snake, which zips out of view and takes your breath with it. Behind you see disappearing the rear of Panapoon, its wide back porches and wispy willow tree swings, its full fish ponds and greasy barbecue pits, its garden sheds and grandparent flats, its determined flowery trellises and reliefs of butterflies aspreading across the rear of every lapboard home, its washing lines flapping with colorful hope.

For a moment it seems you're heading into nowhere via dust and swamp, the last car those wild Handino kids owned appears. Five kids, no hope, as the story goes. That's it, over there on its floored roof, with its black rubbery elephantine ears and a good length of tubing still siphoning off a run of fuel. And there's Kinky Beard's little old river boat, upturned. A "klinker", as they're called. Klunked now. Kinky klunked: a little alliterative story right before us.

And now the road, which has been taking you along the back of the town and behind the hospital, giving you glimpses, keeping you in touch with Panapoonurbia, I guess, opens right up.

There's pavement again, to your surprise, and suddenly a copse, "bearing beautiful chrysanthemums and calamonias" (I lyricize, but yes, some floral adornments, in the dusty overgrowth, a solitary yellow rose, a bunch of pinks). Because here, as you might already have gathered, is the new place where good Panapoonites, aged or assuaged, brought to it from Ward 3 or taken to it from the Emergency Room by miscalculation or misadventure, delivered to it by a high sea or by a low lying bridge, one of the regular salutary medicative fires or, alternatively, one of the occasional pharmaceutical floods. Here, they now end their days.

The cemetery beside the new hospital is a new and growing Town of the Dead. Over there on Row 5, the entire Ramsden family, who not so long ago had spent generations running the steam ship *Leerlane* that chugged up the North Welson River weekly, from the Panapoon sandbar to the upper reaches of Routville, taking fish, tools, milk cans, haberdashery, news, bringing back minerals, root crops, weavings, raw timber and the occasional miner. All of them dead now, from start to finish, along with their boat, brought here one by one.

On Row 6, two tiny dark girls (Milly and Wilda) who, when brought to the coast as babes (last winter, apparently, arriving in a strong sou-wester) had everything in front of them. But, despite this, or because of it, who knows, never made it ("the Typhoid", it is recorded). Enough said. Those sad little cherubs hovering energetically overhead, wings aflapping, heads cocked, in dull white marble, above the tiny humplets of medical suggestion, the old glass bowl and green foam "flower block" atop, the shadow of a kindly old oak, spreading its kindly gnarled arms. I pontificate! Row 13: relatives of Curt Sneed, who propriets the Shoreline (dark rum at 1 shilling, you might imagine, you salty reading coves!), the latter his recently decent wife, Lexie. Row 9, an unknown soldier ("Who?" I wonder. Poisoned by coming home). Row 35, a backblock for timbercutters, fellers, foremen, sawyers, including one man who (quote) "Lost his Life in the Service of the State (? I don't know!). Row 29, Row 27, Row 31, largely fishermen and fishermen's wives. "Laurel Elizabeth Swann, who never failed"; except once, it appears. Died March, aged 57. "Should have lasted longer". William "Pinky" Moffett, Captain of the *Theresa Lynn*, "who sunk in these very waters, 14th July, May the sea keep him in its bosom as he kept his eye so closely on the sea" Too closely perhaps). Rows 38 and 16, adjoining each other at a cross that rises higher than others and leans more than most. The name obscured by rain and wind (why does anyone use sandstone in a monument?). Row 15, heading back toward the unnamed gateway, its flaky trellised overhang of dog rose and dainty green tangles, an archway, somewhat overgrown, through which who knows how many local histories have passed. A tiny stream—some miniscule tributary of The Welson, officially the Welsonette or the Welsonini, no doubt—trickles undisturbed and unrelenting beneath the humped wooden bridge. And out through the arch here to . . .

Well, no! Of course, *look*, I've come unstuck! Some people find it easy to get caught up in time and, succumbing to its somnambulistic tremors fall into such a sleep that the reasons for going anywhere are subsumed into the general flow of this and that so that even before I've got there I'm leaving (mindwise). I once went to Casemont in search of a new propeller and came back with a toaster oven and a tiny pup that the grinning vendor swore was a Terrier; but I found out later, by its unprecedented growth and ultimate displeasure in my company was, in fact, an Shepherd. No matter. Nothing lost. Turn around now, and see there:

Rows 17 through 24. Eight clear, well-kept rows. The sun is lowering onto the beach, on the other side of Panapoon. Waves are lapping against the lapping shore; crabs are scurrying. You get the drift. There's a steady ripple of the Welsonini Stream and the sea breeze that regularly comes in here in the afternoons has seemingly dropped. Through the trees, gently wafting, a sallow, inviting new light. In the distance dogs are barking (possibly out around the old mill), but not in a disturbing way, it's more like a roughhewn song. And the dust that earlier was clogging the hot air has now completely settled, leaving the air transparently glistening. Whereas previously this place had felt forlorn and unfamiliar now, all of a sudden, the combination of light and smell (the scent of the dog rose, maybe?) has changed everything. Some of this might be imaginary, I guess; but powerful, nevertheless. After all, I believe in the importance of fruit to our region. I have grown up in the presence of trees and the family histories of tree-dom. If there is one piece of the past I know to be true it is that piece (the segment, you could say) concerning orchard-ery. But, even allowing for some bias, there's plenty that even the innocent can observe:

Row 17, now there are Apples, four generations. Jermyn, Garwood, Malone, Dorothy, Flora, Nell. Plots close against plots. There's something of a theme: marble grapes (?) draped over a rose stone rise, a clever curlicue of gold along the upper edge of a stony scroll. Each mound rolled and tempered - in couch, it appears; smooth and soft green. After the Apples, Row 18, two ancient members of the Colby dynasty (peach providers for three fuzzy generations; Thomas and Arlene, pa-triarch and matriarch, rest in peace. Ah, too easy a target!). Reliance and Sweet Scarlet varieties.

Row 19: a collection of Donaldsons: all died while tending to their pears and plums. Woody and hardy, as they were. Snows: Row 20. Nectarines. Vazquezes (Vasquezi?); Row 21, A scattering of cherries. Moores: Rowe 22. Jacks of all fruit trades. Row 23: Apricots (Gold Kissed, Nugget). Row 24: Broken Heart Plums, Emerald Beauts.

But, again, I'm avoiding the obvious. It's not so much hiding the truth as arriving, inevitably, at a conclusion. That is - on each stone, whether Apple or Donaldson, Schween, Moore or Colby, Snow or Vazquez or the so far unmentioned Jen-ners, there are highlights of an occupation, and then a hidden, now strangely glowing life (in my medically informed mind at least) pair of dates. Garwood Apple, Chore Boy (Born:

January 26th xxxx; Died this July). Manuel Moore, Flagman (Born: October 2nd xxxx; Died November). Patrick Heppleton Snow, Loader and, latterly, Loader Operator (Born: August 15th xxxx; Died December). Montgomery Donaldson, long diseased, an Irrigation Worker (Born July 12th or 13th xxxx; Died December). Ned Jenn Schwi, Farmer and Wood Turner (Born March 23rd xxxx; Died June).

How true are any of these dates of Life, and of Death?

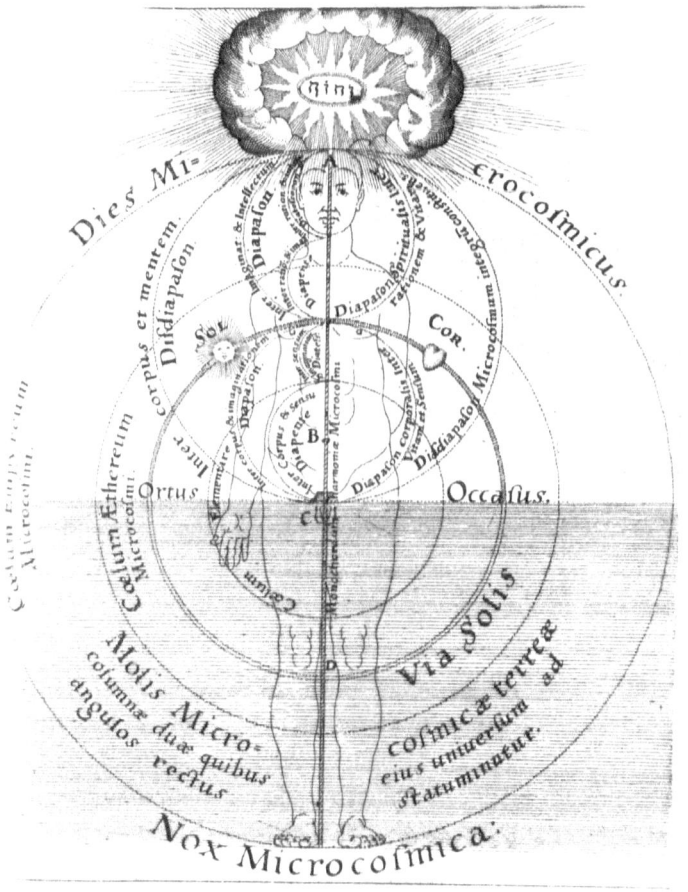

Figure 10.

Death's Arrival I

1.

Propped against the door jam of the Cuuk General Store which, generally speaking, is square, squat, white and right close there by the lolling northern sea of the lolling northern island, the foreign woman appeared to Audie Schwartz to be someone swimming right out of her depth. Grand Audie Schwartz, store owner, trader and fool to his possible last moment!

"So," said Schwartz, addressing Death in that tone he reserved for travelling salesman (those bringing their battered but locked suitcases of enamel dishes, measuring instruments, colorful toweling, floral soap blocks, and the like), up there to the north of the islands, around the tributary or possibly the arbitrary of the Anka River, with its unaffected spiders and languid lizards, its green water tendrils, the ancient travel routes of the Communions for those in search of sea sponges and sea cucumbers, ship wrecks and coral.

I suspect his tone was only one of the things with which Schwartz's visitor took exception. There was in Death's near past—and I discovered this only later, in a long and deep conversation with an absent mainland doctor who I telephoned about our newfound dying and who showed almost no alarm at this announcement (at the time I was otherwise engaged, as I'll mention)—the strained remnants of a confrontation she'd had by telephone with a local agent in Panapoon by the name of Rudd.

Yes, Rudd was living up to his imperious reputation. Formerly of the "Island Divers", so called—some clandestine underwater outfit with dubious foreign connections, I've always assumed—he had tried to recruit the innocent telephoning soon-to-be visitor in the service of "a delivery" (of "medical supplies", apparently, up into the farther reaches of the North Welson and the Anka River, where tribes still dwell happily in the roots of mighty fig trees and visiting scientists are lost, grow bearded, eat their limbs, and become natives—well, so many a distant city newspaper story goes, together with accompanying photographs of the damaged, tanned soul).

Rudd's first (telephonic!) brush with Death! But before the deal had been complete, she had rung off in search of bats and, despite her long reputation for making something out of nothing or, more accurately, for making nothing out of something, now had got lost. For real, or on purpose, who truly knows? She was, after all, no stranger to cunning!

Now I had arrived, spluttering and splashing, in my tiny rescuing sailplane and upset Rudd's poorly engineered cart. No wonder Rudd stood on his doorstep shaking his huge hairy fist at me as I flew out from his jetty. No wonder there was less than the full load in the tank I had paid for. No wonder Rudd would eventually die in a stupor, and a house fire, not two years later. Sometimes everything makes sense. Sometimes nothing does.

"So," said Schwartz, burbling with late afternoon accomplishment and looking out into his front room where the brood of McOrdle children sat, blotching and fracturing before our observing eyes, "You wish to speak to me?"

The general atmosphere of musty contentment, the soft old longues pulled and pushed into their rainbowed disorganization, the posters for outdated slogans ("Yool Honey: It is the Best of Bees"; "Long Live Milk - Live Long on Milk"), the piles of so-called popular magazines, fishing, knitting, fencing (?), and more (donated by reading residents, no doubt), the mahogany trim as dark but as temporary as a chest cold, all these no doubt gave some offence to Death and she took this offence into her squat hard bonnie hatted self so that what Schwartz interpreted as nervous saleswomanship was, in actuality, mortal annoyance and what the squat visitor interpreted as rural ignorance was, in fact, careful personal management of a community of more or less self-sufficient islanders. That's my interpretation, floating above this scene.

If I had really been there even then! If *only*. . . I could have stepped forth from the wings, with my flight helmet flapping and goggles asunder, and a referral to the weather ("By jiminy, quite a storm's a'brewing!") and defused the situation forthwith. But I had my own problems back in Panapoon.

So for now, *enough*! Later. . .

"Speak up! Let me hear. Get on with it," continued Schwartz, in Fateful direction (though at this point I am paraphrasing, not having arrived yet. Maybe all he said, in a careful, studied Schwartz-like way was: "*Yeeees?*").

"No," she replied, and the echo of Death barking that "No" in the small front room started the smallest McOrdle off, coughing and spluttering and making the situation (and their ailments) even worse.

"Oh?" said Schwartz.

Frankly, considering store keepers are bound to converse, that they must communicate in order to sell, that even in the remotest island regions such as these—where tête-à-tête and heart-to-heart are kept to a minimum in light of the particular dangers and threats to good relations between remote peoples, travelers, adventurers, escapees, and the like—even in these regions, amazingly, I find store keepers don't really leave much of a conversational accord.

"I wish to speak to you," said Death (or something remotely like that).

Imagining myself spun up like a spider on the ceiling, I stare down on the two of them, my eight legs firmly placed, my chelicerae (as apparently it's called, scientifically) still, my twelve eyes watching, and I wait for the tale to unfold.

But "Oh?" is all that Schwartz replies, "Oh?" to this squatted be-hatted woman, who is standing there arms akimbo with her boonie hat pushed back, wiping her pinkish brow, looking (though he can hardly be expected to have noticed this) as if she might murder him on the spot.

An awkward disinfectant silence ensues.

"About getting off this island?" suggests Death (again I purely speculate on her exact words)

("How long", you might ask, "is this strange grunting dance to continue?")

"That right?" asks Schwartz, peptically.

Oh please! Give us some relief!

"Utmost importance," portends Death (cutting her words like skin from the surrounds of her bugling throat).

Schwartz, simultaneously, was innocently imagining her suggesting a new range of stainless steel basins set out in size and shape in a shiny foreign catalogue, a stack of dressing pins and blue glass jars, some tin trays and glass cups, a fisherman's bench with smooth ratchet tilting handle, a dozen silvery sponge bowls.

"You don't say?" says Schwartz, in a tone, and with a twitch of his somewhat tall head, that suggested that was exactly what Death did *not* say. Proud as he was, he no doubt took proud exception to the thought of this visitor so desperately wanting to leave the glorious, glorifying islands.

. . .

"A goat got your gourd, madam?" cried Schwartz, or so I imagine him crying with a gourd in his store keeping mind, as I imagine him growing less happy, not least because of the store keepers' penchant for becoming monstrous late in the working day. His yellowish eyes holding a painterly tone not dissimilar to that seen in the inner crescents around an evening eclipse or in the strange hue you find on long worn leather.

And at that moment, as if some heavy philfond lumber had suddenly collided with her from behind, unexpectedly and with its echoically firm grain, Death fell abruptly down on the store floor. Yes, there was Death collapsed right there on that sandy Cuuk General Store floor.

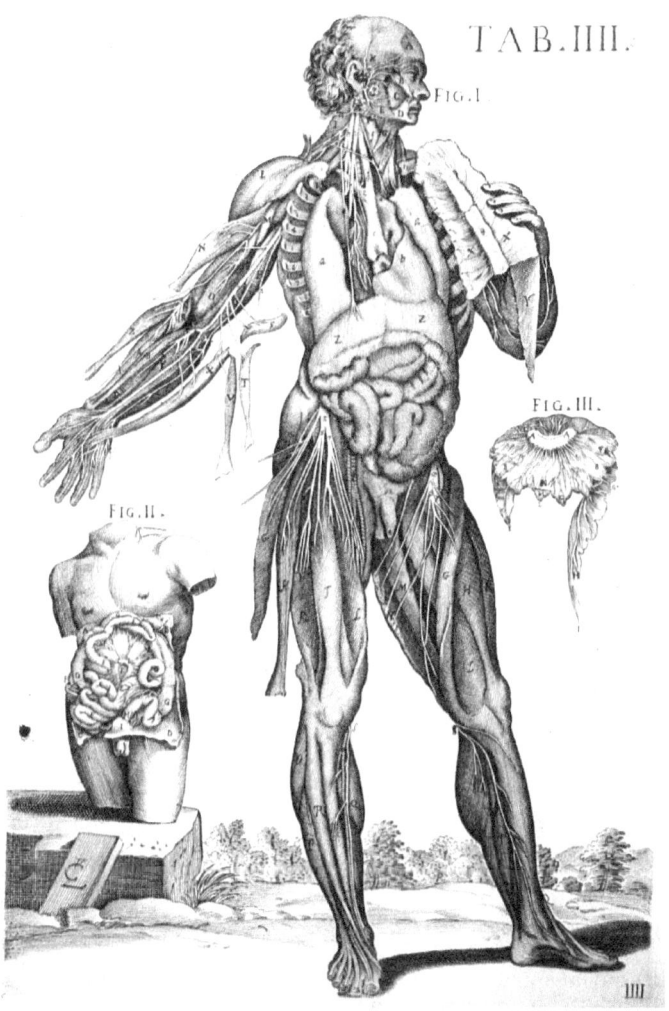

Figure 11. Arriving

Death Rides Again

To cut a long story short, and in that short story make a degree of sense, that is how I came to be assigned to Death. . . . to bring her to the true, bustling Communions (down from her hiding in the north, like a stark cold glacial drift drifting over our shallow warm reefs, you might say). To institute Death here and to be instituted into life by Death too, somehow or other, as if all it took was me alone to change our way of living, alter the course of history, sing her song, sigh her sigh. That kind of thing.

But perhaps I speed along here a little fast!

Simply, this happened, and so did that, and that was the thing, around that moment, and I was drawn, wings spread wide, right on into it.

Because of Death's falling, her exhausted collapse up north, tellingly away from most living islanders. I can't help thinking that she might well have stayed there among the non-existent, if not for me. But because I had once brought a small plane to The Communion Islands, to Panapoon, once shown my entrepreneurial spirit (as some called it), then it was I in Panapoon who could fly, collect Death, and bring her to her new home.

Unplanned and unknown, I was to be Death's temporary assistant, speaking informally and non-hippocratically. The appointment was entirely unofficial! Because I collected her, I was to be Death's guide to us and to our islands, Death's flyer and Death's driver.

"Go!" said Rudd over the phone, me on the tarmac and him at his little wooden card table (or so I envisaged).

"Sure," I replied, and I did, and subsequently brought Death upon us all.

Or perhaps I shouldn't be so hard on myself.

Perhaps Fate played a role. Enormous and timely Fate, clear and present Fate, Fate that watches us and Fate that acts, Fate looking down at me there beside my tiny white prop, beside my long green pontoons, beside my chattering windows, beside my swinging plane door. Or, if not Fate, then certainly Irony—because, given circumstances, me in my plane, her on the ground, me knowing nothing, her knowing everything, me bright and looking to the future, her adrift from her natural moribund habitat, unfamiliar with her island surroundings, looking for some innocent evidence of wheezing modernity to attach her tendrils and from there . . . Perhaps, though, I was only a pawn, a pawn in Irony's game. Irony's fickle thought about us. After all, it was the criminal Rudd who had encouraged her to come here, actually, with all his agenting phone talk of "yes, yes, of course: an enormous colony of bats". He was Death's real agent; I was merely her deliverer.

There I found them, the evening, Death tête with the store owner. She recovering in a cane chair, filthily dressed, sunburnt and worn, bits of the Anka growing greenly over her sodden boots and thick leather leggings. Schwartz behind his storekeeper's desk, in his bright white jacket, looking entirely disturbed. As it turned out, by then Death had been travelling in The Communion Islands, unseen, for over three months. When I picked her up that afternoon in Cuuk, ruddied by Rudd's bat-reporting encouragement and barely awake, she seemed on her last legs herself. A dying Death, spread out across that cane chair so that, though she was not tall, not large at all, the shape of the chair cupped her and taking her disheveled traveling smock, her dirty leggings, her plumped down felt hat, made her a complete landscape there in that chair, her own slumbering world.

Now I accompanied the two of them out the door of the store, into the northern twilight, Schwartz awkward but determined (to get the intruder out of his store, it appeared, though unknowingly. He'd die too, but not yet, not now). Death groggy and muttering, but recovering as we spoke. Had it stopped there. . . . Had we failed to take off. Had we crashed and burned in a tangle of cocoplums and cabbage palms, tangling in vines high on the nearby hill, arms one way, legs another, like spiders blown in. Into a mountain . . . Scattering over the open plains of the lower dividing range. Into the turquoise sea around Skelton Beach.

But no! No, no *no*!

87.

Natus 10 Maii 1591
Obiit Anno 1650

D⸱ GEORG ⸱ NÖSLER ⸱ BERLINENSIS MARCHICVS ⸱
PER ANNOS 32 IN ACADEMIA NORICA PROFES
SOR MEDICVS PRÆSTANTISSIMVS

Figure 12. Me Holding one of the hats belonging to Death

Five Final Hats

1.

Recently, I have inherited from Death five handsome hats. *What?* Purchased by her in Deadtown, Deceaseville or Demiseton, no doubt! All before I ever came in contact with her here in these islands, was made Death's chauffeur and delivered Death darkly right to our door. Either that or these hats were given to her as some pleading offering from the well-known legions of the dying.

I am entirely unsure what to do with this inheritance from Death.

An attorney, stern and professional in his opinion, suggests I might sell each one of them, one by one, in a kind of parade of rippling mortiferous brims and defunctive feathering feathers, but I have no idea what each might be worth, or who might buy such grotesque adornments.

I have inherited this terminant legacy from Death. Death who, in her later years, I did not really know at all—except that she was once Death, and because of that neither entirely with relevance to life nor entirely without it. And she did, I had long known (the hat she was wearing when she arrived still stuck redly with me), possess hats, sun bonnets and the like, to keep her in the disguising dark, and to keep her from our island heat no doubt too, hats she bought later for formal island occasions such as the Parade of Lobster and The Summer Fair; and other, playful, more homely, diminutive hats she bought in her old age perhaps. And thus has arrived this unexpected inheritance.

2.

When this deleterious inheritance was announced I was sitting uncomfortably in an office of a stern attorney in Yard Mile. For those unfamiliar, Yard Mile is a town not twenty miles from Panapoon, small but not inconsequential, slightly back from the sea but not unaware of its pleasant breezes. Well known in banana growing circles, as much of that part of the islands is well known in such cyclical organic local circles. Frankly, I have not spent much time there at all. Actually, to cut right to the chase, I had not been there until I was summoned by letter to this stern attorney's office to hear what Death had left me. And, I certainly hoped, what she intended I should do with these.

You can, of course, think many things in such strange orchestrated moments, such moments concerned with Death that bring about human emotion and memory and pain. For my own part, I thought of aircraft and I thought of automobiles.

I imagined my benefactor, as Death might strangely be called - who I had not seen for some years by then, not at that point had I even seen a recent photograph - I imagined her sitting in beside me in her old black automobile, a dodging decrepit Dodge it was, the kind that once was regularly used here in Panapoon by local gangsters stealing fish and freight and timber, and by the police force alike in the earlier parts of the last century. I do not know much about automobiles, so this first thought was a complete and awkward speculation on my behalf, and not based on anything like great knowledge or perceived fact. Intriguingly, as an astute reader will notice, it combines legality and illegality, which is perhaps telling in some way of what I remember of Death, or what I chose then to remember, as Death came close, and Death moved away, Death became satisfyingly absent, and Death showed herself present again.

My second mechanical thought, inexpert that I most certainly am in most machine matters, except as pertains to small aircraft, was that maybe I had inherited a small red Cessna, a banana duster maybe, something like you might have seen an attractive girl flying in an Elvis Presley movie (should you be familiar with such movies, Saturday afternoons in the cinema here in Panapoon), with a bright blue scarf around her bright blonde hair, a pair of horn-rimmed sunglasses on her pretty flying face, and a deep green banana plantation below. When I imagined this I had my adamantine benefactor now living in a rambling be-porched beach house with a view of somewhere called "Coconut Grove", where "beach boys" on "surfboards" spent time on the sand out front, and there was a grass hut from which you could buy sweet and fruity drinks. But this thought, frankly, only took me so far.

What places were these? What was Death doing in them?

By the time I was arriving in Yard Mile I had left behind my previous imaginary benefactor, one in her black Dodge and the other one who lived at the make believe movie beach and had make believe surfers on the edge of her make believe prim green and tangled garden, and I had taken on yet a another old woman who now drove a pick-up truck which was old and neat, though still green, but the kind of green you see on farm machinery and weathervanes shaped like proud roosters and on bright toy wagons.

3.

At Yard Mile the stern attorney, whose name was Grover—his last name, that is, not his first, and this name belying his forbidding exterior in a light shade of orange, freckled and stripped with age to his skin—explained to me the principles on which my inheritance would be announced.

He said, "I must now explain to you. . ." in a loud, slow and conscientious way that suggested I should not question what came next but simply listen to his low voice and be legally informed.

I was surprised, as you can imagine, that there was no one else there in the room. Urged on by all those hatted women, who in my memory's bright eye had appeared to me as I drove the rattling 20 miles from Panapoon to Yard Mile, I had expected that when I arrived I would find perhaps dozens of those who knew Death, perhaps an entire room full of her discarded acquaintances, jammed into corners on chairs and stools and in huddles, like a mix of complex bereft DNA of Death, unraveled and observable before me.

I had thought that some of these associates and even relatives I might know from photographs and from birthday and holiday cards they had sent to me when I was a young man and they had been attempting to keep in contact with Death, before she moved out of her house overlooking the beach and, subsequently, left The Communion Islands, going off to find work in the Far East, to find her first love, I heard; then later in search of white ice bats (apparently) in the Antarctic or Artic or somewhere similarly frozen; and, later still, in some fatality related medical business—which is no business for the faint of heart, I have to tell you, from experience. I had thought, too, more intriguing than those known acquaintances, even friends, some of whom may have been known to Death by sight and others only by name and place, that there would be others still, who would be more prevalent, and whose appearances and names and places I would not know and whose motivations would be even more unknowable.

Strangely—as if the circumstances were not strange enough already—I had even grown a little protective, as I drove there to Yard Mile; protective, that is, of my former employer, of Death, who had sweetly (if unsettlingly) left me an inheritance, though I did not even know her in her final Deathly days, but who now faced the potential greed, if that is not too strong a word, of who knows how many unknown and possibly uncaring survivors. I had grown protective and concerned and adamant that I would arrive there at the offices of Greely, Grover and White and stand up in defense of now dead Death, whose generosity and brilliance (I imagined myself saying, in her defense) should not now be abused by those who remained here in this world and did not have the same "quality of clear if brutal heart" (a phrase I invented along the way, as my truck bumped and jiggled along the road) as the now dead Death.

4.

As it turned out, I was alone there in the office - except for the presence of Mr Grover.

Mr Grover, stern faced as a bolt head and silvery like one as well, whose second name could have been his first, cleared his throat as if about to set forth along one of those old steam train tracks that make their way out of Yard Mile in the direction of the distant, teeming, raw towns of the Communions' North, hauling a forest of lumber or two hundred tons of prime local corn.

"This, here, is the last Will and Testament . . . ," he began.

"This, here, is the last Will and Testament," he continued, sternly.

I admit I was taken aback by those words. I had not before attended the reading of a Will and was already on edge, because of the recent drive, finding a place to park by his offices in that unknown town, trying to reconstruct a woman who once meant so much but had appeared so little these last ten years, being unsure of who I would meet and what they would be seeking. So these stern words from Mr Grover stopped me in my tracks and I had to hold up my hand.

"Do you need a minute?" he bolted forth in my direction, with the sound like a brick wall hastily erected across those very same tracks.

"I do," I said, trying to catch my breath.

"That's understandable," he replied, somewhat more gently.

5.

I am not one of those rough islanders here on The Communion Islands who have developed a poor opinion of our local lawyers. I am not one of those who believe that our islands' world would be better off without them. I have every respect for our island lawyers, born here but, by necessity, educated elsewhere. It could be said, they are closest of all of us to Death—in their departing and returning.

If not for island lawyers the law here would stand on its own, naked; and as it stood , without the sweater of interpretation and the coat of comparison, without the shirt of debate and the trousers determination, it could well be that island law would catch its death of cold and follow tribal exchange into oblivion. Having island law as sick as that could not be good for any modern islander, in my albeit flighty view. It could even be that the law would itself turn on us and, should it turn on us and invite our green and blue island world to turn on us too, what then? *What then?*

It does not take a great deal of understanding to work this out, a situation as grave and unrecoverable as that. So I am not one who advocates the condemnation of lawyers and the return of the law to its raw, unclothed, original and naked island self. Bring on these foreign-trained lawyers, I say: they are the necessary pressed trousers, the fine silk blouses, the warm and snugly-fitting undergarments in the department stores of the law.

"Continue, Mr Grover," I said, after a moment. "Let's hear what she says."

And so, stern, orange Mr Grover dutifully did continue.

6.

From "Last Will and Testament" to "I direct the payment of all state inheritance taxes" (something Death suffered in her new home, apparently) we were traveling. Onward we went to "and my Estate shall have no right to claim contribution from any person receiving said property".

"What makes a good Will?" I was wondering, there in the mahoganied offices of Greely, Grover and White. On the one hand I meant "Will' in the strict legal sense, not the sense of purpose that the word "will' might more colloquially ascertain in Death's case. On the other hand, I began to think that I meant that too.

"Surely a Will contains a will?" I was unhelpfully thinking.

Mr Grover, meanwhile, was continuing. Indeed, he was nothing if not sternly professional.

"To be reading Death's Will is to be presenting her will," I continued thinking, now gathering in the flow of Mr Grover's words as he gruffly tripped along passages as finally hewn as the statues of long departed island kings and the gateposts of still breathing timber barons. "The will," I continued wondering, "in this case, of now absent Death".

Continued Mr Grover, royally: "To my sister I give. . ."

"Death's younger but less kempt sister, Decay, possibly," I thought.

And so Mr Grover announced a bequeathing of several pieces of unseen jewelry to an unknown and distant sister of my benefactor; unknowingly, as there was still only me present, so what was Decay to know of this?

There followed: a collection of coins and "ancient relics" to a brother named Sebastian (I invent this name as Death did not mention it. He was merely "my brother". Nevertheless, a lost and dilapidated uncle of someone's, I was guessing, who possibly favored a mystery story in a dark wooded sitting room), a small motor boat to the newly commissioned ship's captain (commissioned by Death herself, that is) named Rudd, otherwise more recently the landlubbing owner of the criminally funded "Rudd Transport Inc"; a collection of "household items including my Prevene-Lamport Service" (for the tea connoisseur no doubt) to a Skelton Beach couple, surname of Apple, first names of Penny and Peter fluttering before me. Death was no slouch, it appeared, when it came to collecting recipients, and not discerning about how she went about it, I felt.

When Mr Grover finally reached the part about me, he paused, no doubt to check if I was still there. He had been reading to the paper in front of him for a good hour.

"Are you alright?" he asked.

Except for being tired and curious, I was fine. "Of course," I said.

Then he simply did it: old Death's five hats came brimming my way.

7.

For those who are unfamiliar with inheritance let me say this: when you inherit something on The Communion Islands it does not, generally, as a rule of inky legal thumb, appear then immediately in front of you. This is, of course, particularly being the case when it comes to affairs of property or housing. So, for example, your great grandfather's castle remains where it has always been while you, in the offices high above 9th and Park (or Commonwealth and 31st, some combination like that), look down on the streets below with the mid-afternoon traffic snarled mid-block and the streaming of schoolchildren from the subway and a bus trying to negotiate the protesting members of a Workers Union, and you do not see there your inherited castle, you do not see your turreted and castellated inheritance arriving before you, as if by magic.

I think this general rule of inheritance makes more sense that it first appears. You might think that Rudd would have been pleased to go down into the street and, abandoning his second career as a provider of dubious services, find there his new motor boat roped to a Yard Mile light post. There is merit in this, you say, because then everything is clear, everything is above board. So Deathly Uncle Sebastian, large of beard and larger of belly, is taken into the darkened room opposite and seated before a long polished table proceeds to open his newly-acquired dusty oaken boxes, from which is drawn the golden head of a Pharaoh, a jeweled staff, a bottle of Frankincense, a collection of ivory sewing needles. Or Penny and Peter, Apple by name, apple of your eye by nature, quietly begin to sip their tea from tarnished but otherwise impressive silver cups.

No! Being now experienced at inheritance I know what I would have preferred. I know what my choice would have been. But Mr Grover, professional as he was, had his own ways, ways agreed by him with his partners Greely and White I suspected in the confluence and congruence of case law.

So the door opened. Two women, one small and prim and older, one tall and prim and younger, dutifully stepped in. In their hands were Death's black hat boxes.

8.

"What is a hat?" I ask.

"A covering for your head," you answer.

Oh, how right you are. Ancient or modern, in the cobbled streets of Europe or on the sunny jungle pathways of these Communion Islands, for a standing adult or for a lounging child, on a canoe adrift beside an island, bobbing in the sun, in a coal mine or a diamond cut, at a church, white and wistful, at the fish factory, at rest in a shady bed, flopped, beside the roadside, hard, in a classroom, atop a green mountain, beneath the glass sea, on the paved street, in the warm kitchen, in the wooden garage, beside a railroad as an engine loudly passes, on a ship, on the deck, gold braided, dancing, for a boy on a white beach, saving a life, in a red truck carrying parcels, on a field catching a ball, beside a stream, silver hook in the brim, up yonder in an aircraft, leather flapping around your ears, flowers and fruits on raffia as a song sings, on stage, out in the field, down on the fishing docks, out on roan horseback, across an artillery line, for warmth in a crib. True, true, true, true, true, true, true, true, true, true, true, true, true, true. . .

But what of five hats inherited from Death? Five hats in Yard Mile, five hats in the offices of Greely, Grover and White, five hats brought in, one carrying prim and tall and young, one carrying prim and short and old, five hats on the desk, five hats in black shiny hat boxes, all in a line, now opened.

One, surprisingly, is a silver boater, with a crack in its straw brow; one is a dusty red cloche. One has a feather, long, brown speckled and withered. One is Tyrolean (I think), deep green, with a neat platted band. One, predictably, is a bouffant cap.

"Who," I am wondering, "am *I* to receive these?"

I have inherited five hats from Death. I am unsure what to do with them. I suspect they were purchased by her in Deadtown or Deceaseville or Demiseton, before I ever came in contact with her. Either that or they were given to her as some pleading offering from those legendary legions of the dying. I am unsure what to do with this inheritance from Death.

Death's Story

Still wandering, lonely, mid the funeral urns
To one loved name my saddening thought returns
Less to the many known, but to the few . . .

—*Oliver Wendell Holmes, Lines on the presentation of his por-*
trait to the Philadelphia College of Physicians, April 30th 1892

TAB. VII. ORGANI OLFACTVS. 123

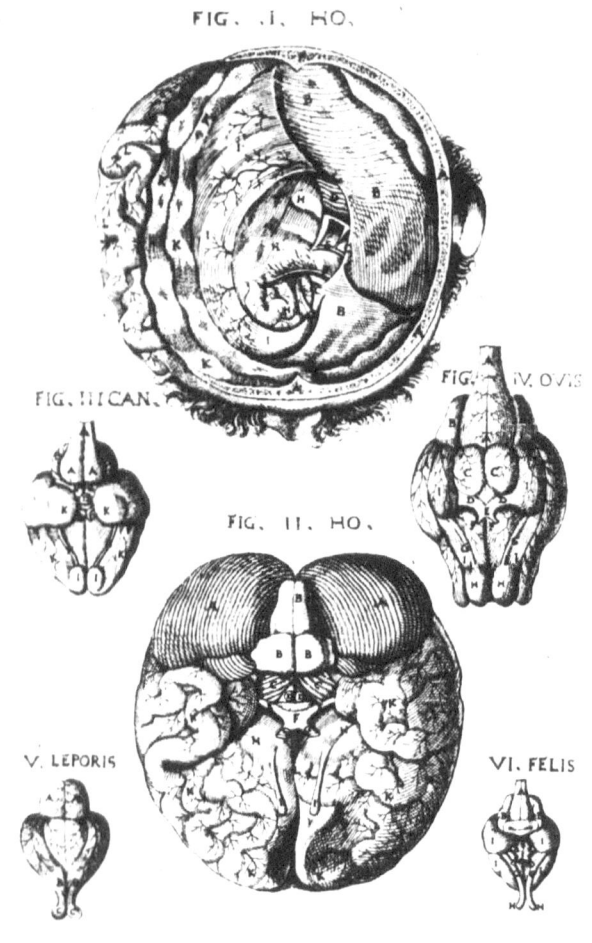

FIG. I. HO.

FIG. III CAN.

FIG. IV. OVIS

FIG. II. HO.

V. LEPORIS

VI. FELIS

P 2   TA.

LUCKY Figure 13.

A Note on Albert Einstein's Brain

My heart in middle age found the Way,
And I came to dwell at the foot of this mountain.

—*Wang Wei (699-759), physician*

February 8ᵗʰ 1971.

I have almost certainly decided to fly to Philadelphia to examine Albert Einstein's brain. It is currently being housed (or maybe that should be "held" there) in that city in the Physicians Museum, as the feisty focus of a global traveling exhibition and I think, at this moment, it will be interesting to consider it. I have to admit, there is something about seeing a brain that distracts me from other things, and Einstein's brain, in particular. I guess you could say that this something I'm feeling is purely curiosity. But that is probably underplaying my real interest and my state of mind, given the brain's ownership and so forth.

Perhaps, in the relative absence of bats and my inconclusive findings so far here, and my sabbatical growing short, what I'm feeling is more like fear.

On the way to the bus for the airport, I'm thinking about that brain and wondering, not incidentally, if that brain is, by wild chance, thinking about me. I imagine that this is entirely impossible; but so far we know so little about the human brain that, "Who knows?" I'm thinking.

If a brain were simply a mechanical device, like an arm or a foot or perhaps a neck, I wouldn't be wondering this at all, or if the bats here had—as was clearly and affirmatively reported by him, Rudd—had they been more prevalent and thus I'd have had other things to occupy me. But we know that the brain is much more than a mechanical device and, if it is more than that, do we really know what it is capable of doing and what it is not capable of doing? What am I capable of discovering, and what I am not.

So I'm considering: what is Einstein's brain thinking about as it sits in Philadelphia in that esteemed Physician's Museum, waiting for those crowds to visit. What is Einstein's brain thinking that I could not, might not ever be capable of thinking, in fact; will never ever *ever* think, even if I might want to?

Could it ever be thinking, as I am idly thinking, that the day here in The Communion Islands is warm and the island children on the white beach here in Panapoon might well be getting sunburnt? Could Einstein's brain have that kind of crazy, almost quaint concern, about children and animals and so forth—much like any ordinary person's brain might possess such thoughts and such thoughts might grow into useful but nevertheless consequential actions, as it were?

Could it be thinking, ever, ever *at all*, about this bright harbor with the bobbling white and red and blue boats and about the islands' fishermen mending their nets and the young girls playing guitars on the park benches, and the blue ibis standing so very still on the muddy sea flats, eyeing the tiny striped greenfish schools by their claws, getting ready to pluck them up, and the waterfalls glistening, as they drop over the red cliffs to the sea, and the golden gulls swooping in long slow swoops over the dark sea, and the water-skiers zooming passed the arched white and pink and yellow and blue façades of the tourist hotels and all the beachfront stores festooned with colored streamers and flags and the like to herald the summer season.

Maybe it is making up all manner of magnificent discoveries, for all I know.

Maybe it is remembering something Einstein once said about the nature of the universe and about how light exists in tiny packets, or something roughly like that, which he liked to call photons, and these packets are tiny chunks of energy, so he said, all of their own, and our universe, these islands, our cities and our towns, even our very homes are all made up of these things.

Or is it perhaps thinking more practically, as I am beginning to think, that maybe I should have driven myself to the airport, instead of getting the bus?

Thought: I am sure Einstein's brain did not arrive in Philadelphia on a bus, but equally I am sure that it didn't arrive there on its own either. With this in mind, someone brought it there and, much like me, it is probably the case that it could not have chosen who brought it there, when and how they did so. That, dare I suggest it, was the product of Fate.

I begin to think Einstein's brain and I might have something in common, after all. I am not thinking this, of course, in any conceited way.

In summer 1967, when I was younger and others were younger still, an unknown and uncelebrated Danish surgeon (dark Dane, I suppose, a secret Scandinavian) by the name of Thorst Handsume discovered during a routine operation that the brain of his patient—a young Communion Islands man who later died in an automobile accident, apparently colliding on the Coral Highway with "a straying coconut goat" [I must check accuracy of this], unconnectedly—continued to emit beta waves, even though the boy was in fact unconscious. This is, scientifically speaking, impossible. The human brain emits delta waves when a person is unconscious, not beta, of course.

Handsume called his new beta discovery "Communions Electricity".

Admittedly, 1967 was a so-declared "crazy time on the Communion Islands" (*Visit Communion Islands*, p.8), as it was elsewhere in the world, I have to tell that reporter. I recall . . . Well . . . In their case, here, distant though these islands are from modern civilization and real world affairs, they are connected to these by seaplane and ship, by cruise liner and tramp, and they were the site of many unusual happenings. Unpredictably, Danish people went there, for one thing, and for no apparent reason. Scandinavians, generally, I've heard. Australians, Greeks, Germans too, mostly. Sometimes these were medical students, during their studying summers. Sometimes philosophers, students of philosophy at least. Sometimes they were musicians—most of The Blend came here, Mott Davis of Green, Alice Koeppner before she did "Journey's Bird'. "It is possible the motivations were related almost entirely to mind expansion" (p.9). Others came from other countries too, sometimes in couples, "with backpacks and books and bandanas' (to directly quote from that *The Trouble with The Communion Islands*, a lively if dubious work about the period). Sometimes alone, with nothing more than a sodden passport and a shimmering smile, I suspect. Sometimes in groups, arguing all the while, as students do. But, famously, they were known here for Handsume's "Communions Electricity".

Handsume published his findings in various journals—the *International Journal of Electroencephalography*, for example, *Neurons and Cognition*; *Telepathy*—where you can still read about them today.

I suspect, as I travel on this bus to the Panapoon Airport, that Handsume's work and Einstein's brain are related.

This laboring local bus is unusually full. Then empty. Then unusually it is full up again, as these proud islanders make their way to the fish factories and the shell stands, to the fruit farms, the hotels and the cafes, to open them, to put out their colored flags and sandwich boards, to scrub at the sidewalks and crank at the striped awnings. The bus moves much like an oxen, first swaying to one side, and then to the other. Passing the time (strange concept!) I imagine each of the heads around me with each of their brains and each of those brains with each of their own thoughts, as the airport bus chugs on down Panapoon Road, then along Skip, then Red Ridge Street, then along Rawley, then past Legros Park, and along Oonapan-panta and then Overton, and Wilberforce and then La Sond, streets I am coming to know here already.

We pull into the airport's grounds just before nine, but the airport is not let fully operational and the terminal is closed until eleven.

"Einstein's brain was removed from Einstein," I tell my-self, sitting here on a rough stump in this dusty parking lot of the Panapoon Airport. "What, then, was Einstein without his brain?" Already dead, of course. But that's not the question.

I'm intrigued, but unsure. I had thought I'd be feeling more excited than this by now.

A Nurse Considers Patients

Thanks for the heavenly message brought by thee,
Child of the wandering sea,
Cast from her lap, forlorn!
From thy dead lips a clearer note is born
Than ever Triton blew from wreathed horn!
While on mine ear it rings,
Through the deep caves of thought I hear a voice that sings

—*Oliver Wendell Holmes, The Chambered Nautilus*

6.00 am. Nurse's Round. Following a slow retreat into a fair sleep last night, putting the light out around eleven - I recorded, faithfully - I imagine this particular bright morning right now to be like the first morning on this Earth. I mean, like it's the first damn morning *ever* that any human has ever been on Earth.

"Ah, monkeys!" you say.

Pretty crazy stuff, huh? Sure. Okay.

It's just so new around here, at the end of the street, overlooking the bay, against that orange Panapoon escarpment, The House wide open for business, and with all the others around me looking so damn positive, that the end of my first full month -------

Well, any first morning is easy enough to imagine, given that at some point there has to *be* a first morning, and given that in this place, on the main island also, everything seems much closer to its origins in my view, or whatnot.

On the first morning ever ever *ever*, I just imagine a human being stood up.

"Look," it said, to no one.

No one was there.

But, sure, they looked out over some lava like plain, scientifically speaking, with those too bright browns and oranges and those deep hard impossible reds, flowing in front of them, that not quite molten ashen rock and those ginormous bits of tree and whatnot, and they said to absolutely no one:

"So now it begins."

"So it begins," a first human said.

That's easy enough to imagine.

"So now it begins. Now *what*?"

Then you cannot, of course, help yourself but imagine when it all will end. That's the point. Something that begins has to have an ending. It makes sense to me. Unless, of course, that thing you're talking about is so-called "perpetual motion" — which it's not, whatever that actually is, medically.

Today will end. Tomorrow will end. Eventually a day will end and no other day will start. "Endings", by Lord "will beget the mighty ending"—to speak biblically or whatnot.

I don't know. Have you ever considered death?

Have you ever considered death?

7.17. Nurse's Round.

Life, I guess.

The universe—everything beyond, everything around and everything, everything, every crazy thing you can ever or will ever see or imagine—the universe is *not* in forward motion, constantly going on and on and on and on and on and on and on.

It's not something that continues, indefinitely, forever, like an overbalanced wheel or like a capillary bowl, rolling, or pumping along every single damn moment of every single damn day of every single damn year, forever and ever.

That contradicts the basic, irrefutable laws -----

I shouldn't have said that.

8.45 am. Nurse's Round. More focused when you wake.

Endings make beginnings, damn it. That's why the universe will end. That's why we (me, you, everyone here) have to end. That's why having an ending must be, and is ultimately good, frankly.

Endings matter, that's all.

Frankly, if the universe was not going to end it would have had no damn place in beginning, in my personal view anyway. It would have made no sense to start.

Knowing that it will end is -------

If I look around at maybe Cxxxx, ALICE, and Fxxxxx, KAT and Mxxxxxxx, HASUKI, Exx, ALVIN, maybe some of the outer islander kids: Yxxxxxxx and Cxxxxxx, skinny baby Txxxxxxxxxxxx, I see in them their hopes.

That's all I mean.

A first morning would have been like this.

9.07 am. Nurse's Round. Harold is really *really* guarding his entrance today, I notice.

Some expanse of island territory, and though these islands are all green and blue and the mountains in the distance are not smoking, not volcanoes, and there are no giant screeching lizards falling hopelessly into some kind of flaming mess.

But, otherwise, it would have been exactly the same as this.

Is this a new "Hospital"?

A "Medical Center"?

"The House". I don't know.

Harold, some of the patients are already calling "Chief" something, or "Head" something.

"The Nurse's Office" he calls my room, and when he calls it "The Nurse's Office" he calls it that with such a clear, deep sense of local pride.

Much about Harold is proud and hopeful. Not boyish or chubby—to be a little unfair, truly.

'Ah monkeys!" He's just turned 22. In Harold-years, as I have come to call them, meaning days or months he's survived here, but made into his real years, so that his time now is his whole lifetime. If that makes any sense!

Sitting at the front door with the key in his hand (accurately, I think that should probably be "Key"—because it is for the single ownership of Harold, that big old Key) Not that Harold has to lock anyone in around here. The patients are all here of their own free wills; or because, to be honest, their parents probably used to tell them those stories of when the Communion Islands was a place of disease and despair or whatnot, and ----

"Disease and despair," they call it, that period in island history (*History of The Communion Islands.* p.43) No one then lived long, it's widely and repeatedly written, though no records were kept so it's hard to say how old they lived properly, or how accurate the stories are. But now, of course----

Modern medicine. Everyone lives much longer. And here, they say, if we can finish our work building medical care "here on the Communion Islands", and whatnot, they all might live longer still.

"Forever maybe", says Pxxxx, in Bed 13, which is about as crazy a notion on these islands ever had.

"It's true!"

Even Rxxxx, whose parents apparently run a touristy tour boat out of Skelton, make a packet, and seem to be well grounded in daily life, doesn't immediately disagree.

9.48 am. Nurse's Round. Baby Harold looks so helpless that I feel like planting one on his enormous brown cheeks, or running my fingers in his hair, up over the meaty rim of one of those giant Harold ears.

That Key in his hand could be a stick some kid is using for wheeling a lobster cane—in that time around here when kids did that kind of thing for fun. One of those big lobster trap hoops that rattled around with kids screaming along behind them, whooping and laughing, before they caught some disease and went and died, I guess. Though not to be morbid. And times change.

Harold's hair flops all over his baby head, over his baby eyes. 22 days. How much longer does he have?

I call out: "Harold, I'm leaving."

He looks at me with his usual unbelieving, hurt Harold expression, and taps his big Key on his big fat knee. He counts the other patients in, he counts the other patients out. So far he's just counted them in, to be accurate.

"Nurse?" he says.

When Harold first arrived I thought he was much older, or maybe it was that he was as old as he ever was going to get, I mean, I suppose.

No older, no younger, so that he appeared to me in that new examination room to be fixed in place already here, as sturdy as the thick metal tubing on the bright yellow wall.

Looking out to sea ---- it's as if around the headland will come that famous old Communion Islands hospital ship, *The Lady Florence*, her tattered sails all ablaze with sunset and her aching decks swarming with sick kids, shuffling up against those railings. I mean, that's what it's like, given that the purpose of the hospital is to deal with "the appalling state of islander health" (*Communion Islands News*).

11.01 am. Nurse's Round. If the truth be known.

What all islanders do on the Communions Islands, regardless of whether it is good for their own well-being or not, and because it is necessary and almost real, is to trade in a modern human fantasy.

What all islanders do on the Communion Islands is trade on a fantasy that one day a visit right here will solve all the entire collective boredom of the entire collective damn modern world.

What—that no one will ever need buy a ticket to anywhere else but here, ever again, that being.

No chasing some silver plane down a runway sobbing that your ma or your poor demented great aunt is going off somewhere you aren't so sure about. No bringing down those piles of photos from up in your roof and collapsing in a carpeted chair, faded old photos around, and some other kid cousins at some -----

A ragged beach in some other tropical place, probably! Competition.

Some other Christmas tree place, some other Christmas tree place, after other Christmas tree place.

Holding up pictures beside of trips somewhere "for the sun", or whatnot, or that one time, one year, your Dad tried to take up jogging instead and almost killed himself on the street outside. No softly spoken "Sorry you can't be here" bouquets at the door, from world cities with world addresses. No solemn foreign taxi drivers. No glassy airports.

You'll never have to wait for a transfer to *any*where for God's sake. Come here.

Hey, there's no need to stay home and join rows of the unknown in silent stupefied unquenchable

Boredom is a killer!

How is your local museum? What speech are you going to your local club, your old school or ----.

Girl scouts, I guess, talking about their "last great hike to -----"

The Communion Islands!!!

We trade here on life. Because in life we have everything.

"From the sea to the mountains" we say (or our brochures do, for starters).

"Snorkeling."

"Deep-sea Fishing."

"Travel the mountain tram!"

"Pick a Pineapple".

"Watch the local islanders make a basket".

Need I go on? The last thing anyone can be here is *sick*! Heaven help us.

Midday. Nurse's Round. Harold again.

"Harold," I say, as he sits in his strange little room he's turned into a kind of stall, like a kid managing a ticket booth at the cinema.

"Harold, I'm leaving. I'm going to get a drink. I'm leaving right now."

The patient in Bed 4—Harold that is—stands up, exits from the rear of his stall, and wanders to the edge of the paving stones, as if beyond that he will turn into a pumpkin or some other magical giant Harolding thing.

"Do you hear me, Harold?" I call from the hallway, propping against the wall.
    "I hear you," says Ixxxx, in a slow graveled whisper, from the doorway of the nursery nearby, a thick curl of her golden hair curled down between her lips.

Maybe I can count on Ixxxx. She would come, if I just up and went.

If I said "Let's leave this dying behind" then off we would go, she and I. "Let's get away from this dying, huh?"

Up north, where the islands are still becoming new, somehow, and Death is still largely unknown. Up there Ixxxx might live, Harold might live. They all might live.

"You know," I say, not to Ixxxx exactly but to the air around her, "if we left tonight we would make it to Clear Lake before he would even notice."

Which would be a cure in itself. Me like a pirate with a motley not forever dying but never dead crew. That kind of thing.

Carcinoma. She's from Cuuk, apparently. Her father's an officer of the police force.

I watch Harold wandering out onto the trimmed green grass. Green green *green*.

You can grow anything in this dirt. Long past volcanoes and their mighty flows have left all this. The soil's a colorful swirling mess of orange and yellow and brown. Constant ebb and constant flow, you know?

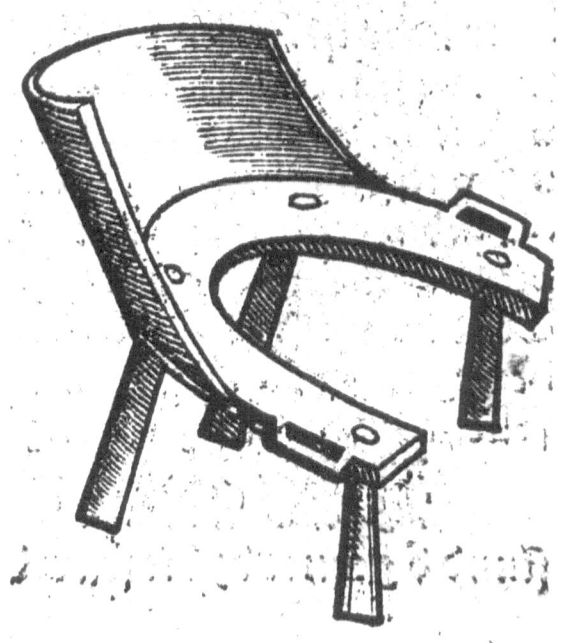

Figure 14. A Birthing Chair

Death's Story

Next to the wound, what women make best is the bandage.

—*Barbey d'Arrenville*

The well-trained physician knows what to do for his patient. The exceptionally well-trained physician knows what not to do.

—*Sydney Smith*

What tho' the art of healing we pretend,
He that designs it least, is most a friend.
Into the right we err, and must confess
To oversights we often own success.

—*Sir Samuel Garth,*
The Dispensary: A Poem in Six Cantos (1750)

Making the Hospital

1.

If you have no real interest in the material *and* immaterial significance of modern medicine, the joining together of flesh and future, nerves of steel and constitutions of stone, good health in patterns of human behavior as significant as the weather and as everlasting as Eustrucus or the flow of white sand over the magnificent Ampool Plain of the Communions Islands, then there is no point in having a conversation with a woman such as myself.

Modern medicine fascinates me. I like to bob down, or reach up, at the sight of it, whichever emerges from shiny medicinal logic, and run my calloused fingertips over its various germ free surfaces. The medical types and institutional intentions intrigue me. The smells and colors of medical manifestations, patterns of movement of wheeled and shuffling patients, the arrival of relatives, the liveliness of staff, human texture as it might be called, shapes of hospital institutional light and clinical sound, whether out in the terracotta mountains of the Communions or on the marble steps of Oxbow and Golders School of Medicine with its fine, bleached porcelain and ancient anatomy theaters.

A thing descends. Call it curiosity. Call it carnality. Call it primacy, I guess. I believe the types and combinations of modern medical care are infinite, and its very existence is the substance, the making, of hope and human ambition. I have a feel for it all.

The Communion Islands was one example.

Now there was an opportunity that would change a life. It was an opportunity a woman could dream about forever and never come close to occupying. *C'est d'accord.* Women do dream of such opportunities, I know, because I've had women say to me:

"O, I envy you, the work you do."

I work, of course, no different to any other woman, I find, having had periods of concentrated devotion, lapping against days of complete and utter disinterest, the ebb, the rush, a trickle of possibility, making the flow of good and bad which is an ordinary life. Dead though I now am, I have no complaints.

Fate had it declared, and the declarations of Fate are not to be taken lightly, that modern medical care would come to The Communion Islands. And so I had it in my mind to over-see its creation, to be the project's island medical advisor. The island ways were such that news traveled fast and such news, laudably, traveled honestly.

The post of "Medical Officer" was advertised in the February edition of *JBMA* (Romantically, I like to believe it was the Leap Year issue). I was on the islands in pursuit of my bats, wrong footed by a fool who knew nothing about bats, and read the advertisement in my ragged copy over a fire of sticks and stones and few other possibilities. My prospects so far were low, and my successes limited.

The next day, slightly buoyed, I submitted my letter of interest on my makeshift letterhead, all nicely typed in my new bamboo hostel room, prim and plumb, and addressed, as was required, to The Clerk, Communion Islands Government Offices. I had yet to sight those offices in Panapoon, or

Red Ridge Street, or the Office of Fisheries and Shell Fisheries and the Office of Roads and Mines, or the Office of Island Records and the Office of Tourism and Air Transport, or The Clerk himself. My time in the Communions was still short.

I had been up north, around Cuuk and Complexion, or some version of that, around and about, searching out, thinking, wondering what to do next. If not for the presence of *Cynopterus sphinx* and *Megaerops ecaudatus* I'd have probably gone mad. For better or worse, I had been working up until my arrival on The Communion Islands, and for want of a proper alternative, at a private health spa at the London home of a certain reclusive singing star, whose name I would mention if not that it would make it sound like I'm big-naming myself, which I'm not about to. My penultimate medical job, as it turned out.

Suffice it to say that the high glaze on his floors and the height of his ceilings would have substituted for those big wall mirrors reflecting the great man up, down and sideways and that the main bedroom had a solarium and a gymnasium overlooking 'the bay' or, as he called it, the "Hen Harbor".

I'm told he was quite a brilliant local soprano before he matured but, by the time I made his acquaintance, he had long left Europe to make his name and subsequently returned, so named, and was big enough to house three sopranos in that skin that house one wheezing, lecherous tenor. Officially, I was "on sabbatical" from his job, as this notion seemed to thrill "Mr Una Furtiva Lagrima" that he could giveth and he could taketh away. But I had it in mind not to return. I had it in mind very much.

A week passed. Ten days. Eleven. I began to give away the idea of staying on the islands as a lost cause, and was about to head back to the mountains in one final search for *Nyctimene Albiventer* and *Paranyctimene Raptor,* or what I thought was possibly a colony of *Balionycteris Maculata*, or could have been, based on what I thought I'd seen, stripes and furtivated snouts and the like. Though, frankly, it could have been *Thoopterus Nigrescens*, for all I knew really. I hadn't yet got close enough to truly find out. I had enough money for one more trip to the north and a thought, as thoughts go, that if I could find the colony I could study them and if I could study them, who knows? Failing that, or following that if needs be, I could return to London and there, grit teeth, tend to the tender tenor, and build up my resources again.

Next thing, however, I received a call to come down to the hostel desk and found there a letter in the morning post saying:

Dear Applicant,

Subject to below, I am pleased to advise that your application for the provision of the previously listed services has been accepted. It is required that, as this is a position of trust, you should confirm that you have are not subject to legal process or conviction, subject to disqualification of license or that you are currently under investigation, probation or similar for any breach of the law. Following receipt of confirmation, I look forward to meeting you and to seeing work undertaken within the dates fixed in our schedule.

Sincerely,
Clerk
Communion Islands Government Offices

Naturally enough, despite what I had been hoping, this sent me into a spin. I couldn't simply up and leave the tenor's spa in favor of the clerk's islands, no matter how much I wanted to do so. For one thing, the tenor had a naturally elided temperament, the kind that sparks and spurts and eventually causes you financial trouble. I was in my first medical post for quite some time, who knows what damage he might do! (and I might do too, to the general world of music, if he was as good as claimed). For another thing, I was having a hard time convincing him to pay, even when he was at home. "Tenor or tenner?" I wondered, to be crass. I was running short of funds.

And then, of course, there was the other thing, the small matter of a brief court appearance when I was a tad younger, and my subsequent five months imprisonment.

The matter was a misunderstanding only. I had met a young man in a remote mountain village of an even remoter Far East nation, name unmentionable. Taken him home on horseback, so to speak. Made certain promises, informed by my maturity and directness. Suggested particular possibilities. He had turned out differently. Accused me of treating him badly. Made various comments on my character.

I protested. He threatened. And the matter ended up in a local court.

I said to my lawyer, who was the best I could afford at the time and mostly good at his work, "Sir, it was love at first sight." Being more of a pragmatist than I, he laughed rather raucously; but I assured him I was serious.

I had seen this young man standing by a fountain in the local town square. The water. The sun. The burble of voices. Who would not be moved? My heart elected to follow a route I could not alter. I introduced myself. He said my name was a proud one. Sweet. A man of his time, I thought. I invited him home. He accepted, and seemed suitably firm in the saddle. Thus I was led to believe that the feeling was one we shared. On arrival at my forest door I told this young man that I'd fallen in love with him that very afternoon and would only wait for an appropriate moment at which to propose marriage. He dismissed this as sweet but unusual and said that we should get to know each other a little better first. That, of course, was the first sign that we were unsuited. Afterwards I discovered that he care more for my promises than about my reasons for making them.

Whatever his motive—and I never wasted time in questioning it—the case reached that court of a Magistrate called __ (names elided to protect the guilty), who was then a man renowned for his level-headedness, and a rather large pair of green eyes, incidentally. All the better to see his cases with.

I was pleased to be judged by such an eminent man, and told him so at the first opportunity, for which I was duly censured by the young man's lawyer, who seemed at the outset determined to make me a travelling criminal.

I told my story exactly as it had happened, leaving out a small section on my search for a colony of *Dobsonia Chapmani*. For that the young man's lawyer accused me of being a liar.

"Oh, this is *too* much," I cried, naturally, and banged my fist down on the redwood desk, in order to get my message across. He then immediately accused me of being unbalanced. A comment that had me threatening to blacken his eyes.

"You do not know me!" I shouted. By this stage, against my previous predictions, the young man himself had bizarrely taken to blubbering loudly into his hands, and the whole courtroom was fairly soon unable to hear my defense. So I called to the magistrate:

"If justice was to be done I must be allowed to explain the reasons for my actions," I said.

And, of course, of subsequent offer, which now seemed out of order, I agreed, but he had not come to me, after all, in his current blubbering state. Had he done so, all wet and shuddering things would not have proceeded as they did.

By then the magistrate, first name of Flounders or Findus or the like, was banging his own desk (a large oaken, by all outward appearances, and handsome) with his black gavel and he'd turned a healthy shade of pink. He abruptly offered me five minutes in which to conclude my defense.

I am not one to miss an opportunity honestly offered by a magistrate, especially an eminent one, with all that eminence entails, in history and in jurisprudence, and the like.

The beauty of that town square in Spring, I explained, with its hedges of wisteria, mauve and white and hanging in grapely splendor—how about that? And the carpet of native pansies—an indigenous pansy carpet, laid there—petals flapping like velvety *Pteropus Woodfordi* in the light mountain breeze. And that?

I said, naturally, quite naturally, that the young man, the same young man who now blubberingly accused me, had enhanced the beauty of the place with a milky beauty of his own. I made it clear, and clear it certainly was, that when the young man stood by the fountain he seemed to me to be a young man waiting for my arrival as I had long been waiting for his.

"Appearances," I said, "as many will attest, are often everything."

I recalled our first glance at each other, him in his place, me in mine, and how our eyes fixed through a haze of Spring northern heat (not unlike that experienced in the upper reaches of the more famous hillsides around The Communion Islands' town of Panapoon, incidentally). And remained fixed as I approached him. On the ride home, I said, I did not speak, as if in our new world there was no need for words or any other language, graphic or suggestual or otherwise, all being encompassed in "our presence together". How grand this would be. And a nice turn of phrase, I thought.

"We were one," I said, "by the very force of love itself."

I have to say, though it came naturally to me to speak this way, I could hear among the court audience the first small volleys of their dissent. It might have been the translation facilities, I thought, which were rudimentary at best in those parts.

Suffice it, there were coughs and, to accompany these, there were grunts: the kind of thing that gets your dander up, if you know what I mean, especially in important circumstances. Nevertheless, going on . . . I recalled how when we arrived at my home, which is modest but not unattractive and to be taken exactly as it is, with its display of nectarous plants and the like, the young man seemed entirely familiar with his surroundings and, to my surprise, me entirely comfortable with him flying around those surroundings, and inspecting them. As a courtesy I asked him:

"So, then, tell me: what's your name?"

First name only, I insisted because even then, frankly, I did not wish to imagine him having a lineage other than that he would soon share with me.

By now, to my surprise, some of the court audience was twittering with laughter. A woman can take so much, I have to say, and this, after everything else, was turning my mood. I stopped my defense and, controlling my tongue, nevertheless turned on them and asked them if they would please allow me the opportunity of using the magistrate's full allotment to me.

"I cannot think straight," I called out to them.

With that, two rotund tiger-shadowed men in the back row, stone cold killers I suspected, shouted in unison that I probably had not done so for some time. What, I wondered, had overcome these two?

I did my best to ignore these stout golden bookends and continued, recording only in my careful outline my feelings, where truth always dwells of course. I did so, despite the guffaws that followed, which sounded not unlike the mating call

of the *Desmalopex Leucopterus*. Cooowhip! Cooowhip! Needless
to say my allotted minutes were quickly being used up.

The young man who had accused me, I said, had given
himself over to me in every fashion imaginable. "*Every* one," I
said, and I could hear the change immediately, in that volley-
ing audience. In his scent, I said, for starters, which was reminiscent of barley, and the obvious warmth that comes from
that, and cave moss and, finally, peaches.

The audience, I realized, was now filling with chatter.

In his voice, I told them, which was inquiring in that way
of voices that do not know their place or that do not assume
their inabilities but that reach out from a person so that they
are like a hand placed, so. That was his voice. So. And in his
eyes, I said. Oh, his eyes I said, so that were they really windows they would not ever be able to stop the light that spilled
from the outside world to inside, inside to outside, and there
in those eyes, which were indeed wide wide open, you could
see more than any vista I had ever seen.

"Ho!" the young man, suddenly cried. "I gave you nothing!"

"Oh, but you did!" I replied. And despite my prim though
economical local lawyer's instruction to now keep quiet and
let legal process prevail, I could not help myself. "You gave me
a great deal," I said.

"Ho! Ho!" my nameless suitor shouted. "Ho! Ho! How
dare you say such a thing?"

"At first," I replied, "I was quite taken by it."

By now, admittedly, I felt the magistrate was beginning to
lose control of proceedings. The young man had a number of
friends and they had each in turn risen from their seats in the
front row, thinking their nameless friend in need of defending. Of defending, that is, from *me*. Me, who was no more
or less than a reasonably mature and educated woman, who
had taken on the task for loving a younger man for his ben-

efit as well as for any benefit of my own. Who had seen the signs and, in the natural way of signs, been directed by them. But his friends—because that's what they were, associates, compatriots, conspirators—his friends said that his honorable name had been besmirched.

"The rules of love," I said, in a decidedly calming and mature voice, "are quite plain."

"Look," I said, turning to the gallery where the seated looked perplexed and the standing looked indignant.

Above and beyond, through a skylight, I could see sparrows flocking in the bright Spring frangipani trees.

"I'm sorry it didn't work out," I said. "I really am. But, frankly, we were at odds. You have no idea."

"Well, well," cried one of the young man's friends, of the indignant group, which had grown larger. "So what is wrong with him then?"

"Wrong," I said. "Not a thing!"

The sparrows duly chirped, as sparrows do.

"Nothing at all," I repeated. "I merely say that what he offered didn't suit me."

With that the young man broke down completely. His friends, the indignant, the few who remained seated, all of them, turned to him, in his seat. His escarpment friends, the perplexed, looked down from above. I do not know what the sparrows did, as the magistrate had begun banging his gavel, *plop plop plop*, and I could not easily extract myself from the scene around me.

"You are vile!" cried the young man, or a word like "vile", but something from his local dialect.

"Vile, vile, *vile*," he blubbered, dialectically. How could I have deceived him that way? He asked. How could I have tricked him into going with me? What had I been planning? What delusion was I under?

Now the sparrows returned to my defense, bless them. *Chirp chirp chirp.*

I tried to calm the gallery, I turned to the magistrate, whose gavel had paused momentarily in respect of the scene that was unfolding, and possibly of Spring, which had brought to the trees quite a lime green gloss, so that as the sparrows flitted to and fro the glitter of each adaxial surface spread near and wide. I know a thing or two about new foliage, needless to say.

I had not tricked him, I told the gallery. "Not at all", I said, to the judge. Our agreement had been mutual.

"Why, indeed?" I said. "Why would he have come along, otherwise?"

It was point well made.

How could I have led him?

Me? No.

"Your honor," I said, almost at the end of my time. "Our agreement was *mutual.*"

"You prig!" screeched a girl in the audience. That very same girl, small and neat and unexpectedly loud, who hid beneath an enormous pink hair bow.

"Your honor," I said, trying to ignore that intrusion of that bow. Hadn't I returned the young man to the very spot where we'd met? Hadn't I wished him well? Hadn't I sat with him there, after all that had happened, despite all that had happened, and spoken about the future? His, mostly, that is. Hadn't I said—and I turned now to the gallery, upper and lower, the red bowed girl, the alabaster brothers, the skeptics, the voyeurs, the principled, the indignant, the seated, the ringers, and the sparrows beyond, who only judge what they see and who had grown quiet but for the slight ruffling of feathers in the slight Spring breeze—hadn't I said, carefully, kindly, that his substantial gifts, his good looks, his careful

eyes, his smooth skin, would find much support, "nay, grati-
tude, in fact," I said, from someone, other than myself?

"Your honor," I said, "now at the end of my time, "I leave
it . . . with you."

To decide my fate, that was. Strictly speaking, what more
could I say? Legal process is its own master, or mistress, if you
hold to the ancient idea.

"My relationship with the young man was as genuine as
circumstances allowed," I concluded.

Figure 15.

A Treatise on Doctors Not Found in The Communion Islands

Exhibit 1.

As opposed to the traveling doctor such as me (experienced generalist who heads to the site of medical action and need) a medical specialist, the young city doctor (as I call him—they are notoriously male) will walk with arms firmly tucked against his sides, to avoid making human contact. A sound like a light sawing of soft timber will paradoxically emanate from his presence, though seemingly not from the mouth, as his lips will rarely open or move at all. How he speaks to his patients is beyond me! The young city doctor will not have true facial expressions, in fact barely any facial expressions at all other than the informed yet vacant look of someone neither confident that they want to exist in our world nor sure they must certainly exist in another. The young doctor will crave friendship, yet will always, I've found, shy away from it.

Exhibit 2.

Do not take personally that handsome young doctor's failure to accept your casual invitation to drinks or a meal. Apparently such a young doctor rarely ever eats and he rarely ever drinks. Though he may recognize familial exchange, it is the exchange of vibrant city life that he really understands and requires. Everything else is only a passing circus-like distraction, as his is apparently a medical intention far more important than daily life, far more significant than any one yawning issue of rash or cough or playground injury, an urban satisfaction more compelling than mere suburban or country or universal life beyond. He is rarely distracted from his metropolitan offices.

Exhibit 3.

Such a young doctor will not entirely recognize friends or former lovers when he is in the throes of his work, except for a brief moment (on which more, in a moment)—though all is not lost. A young doctor, full of singular city intentions though he appears to be, will frequently respond to unexpected sound, such as the accidental kicking of a newspaper stand as you rush to catch him, or the overly loud c-l-o-c-k of a steel door as you flee out the back of a stairwell in his building when embarrassed by being found there. Equally, while his own communicative repertoire will be limited to individual variations on the general theme of grunting and yowling at the sight of we mere shuffling humanity, this will not prevent him responding to your own manifestations of humanness with a passing,

"Doctor" in the corridors of the Metro Memorial, Internal Medicine.

Suffice it to say, your shouting out or screaming in frustration at his professional and personal detachment will, inevitably, only make the situation worse, with the steady rise of human sound seeming to create in even the least attentive young doctor a revulsion equivalent to your own discovery of a large black spider in your bed or stepping on the regurgitations of your ailing old cat. Crying, on the one hand, will create in this doctor a manner of inquisitive determination and he has been known to claw their way through the roofs of wine cellars or the double-bolted doors of padded bedrooms to escape the mere hint of weeping.

On the other hand, young doctors find joy, and the laughter that accompanies it, unfathomable and they pause at the sound of it, with their heads turning to the side and their sometimes well exercised but strangely uncoordinated limbs suddenly stiff in anticipation. A young doctor's interest in laughter is seemingly an unconscious craving for something more, some central component of his hidden character, contradicting any passing notion that this doctor lacks full human consciousness.

Exhibit 4.

This "craving", as I might call it, is one of most notable and yet least understood of young physician traits and, despite the work of such eminent medical theoreticians as Montgomery, Spivak and Tatiani, little is truly known about how the true specialist differs from the rest of us. As supposedly he does, and will reiterate this himself.

Montgomery suggests: "a developed practitioner seeks out people because she or he sees in their situation a remnant of their former non-medical life, alongside the recognition of their future one". While Spivak, whose analysis of the day-to-day lives of catatonics and Psychogenics has also been universally well received, counters with: "in dealing with specific medical issues in a specific way, which is a physical and psychological attribute as well as moral in nature, the specialist practitioner intends to declare that which makes up a particular condition and the condition he observes around him". "Either way", suggests Tatiani, who is the youngest of the three speculative medical historians but was recently appointed as the distinguished Chair of Medical Ethics, and appears to be already presiding over it with his young iron hand: "in this act, which is both spontaneous and spectacular, the specialist physician seeks something of our own heightened temporality. He is, metaphorically speaking, on a time-clock."

Exhibit 5.

Tick, tick, tick! Fascinating! So that's it?

It might thus be said, a young doctor will participate in acts of both sound and vision, but that his sound and vision is not necessarily my (or your, of course) quiet, controlled, nonintrusive own sound. He will walk with his deep clear eyes fixed with impossible concentration, straight ahead, not veering to one thing or another as I, or you, might. He will not be distracted by the entirely valid lives of the others around him, but only by the intrusion of sounds and sights of shock or other heightened medical states of the Emergency Room that match, at least in some way, his own heightened state of self.

If forced to go into the countryside (by a senior class invitation, say, where Charlie Thompson was a challenger and real jock, say) he will climb no fences and adhere to all boundaries of farming properties; while, in the city, he will frequently be found in the foyer of hotels and "headquarters" attending to textile magnates or the owners of warehouses and stevedoring firms that, while repulsive to those of us who live in the clean, real world, seem to carry for him some suggestion of travel or transit that best matches his medical ambitions.

Exhibit 6.

Finally, and I've been amiss: that brief moment I mentioned. Such a physician will not recognize love, except for a brief moment when they are not thinking about the Hematopoietic and Lymphoid class. In that moment they will encapsulate all manner of tenderness, devotion and fondness in such a way that no one before them or after them will ever encapsulate it so well again. Their eyes will soften, where usually they are glaring; their shoulders will relax; their steps will grow smoother, less staggering, more sure. You will swear at that point that their arms will reach forward and grasp their love with such adoration that no force in the world will prevent it. But then, at the moment of seeming climax, right at that moment, their movements will change, and the sound that emanates from them will grow louder and they will thrust themselves from side to side in a manner reminiscent of someone in battle with a tornado or with the buffeting of a space rocket, and they will fling themselves past you, their head shaking violently. And, at that moment, should you catch sight of that future old doctor's face, you will see there, as if on a canvas, a deadpan clarity, a longing for something unfathomable that will shock you.

Medicine and love are, in so many ways, one and the same.

Figure 16.

Holoquet, The Anka River, The Communion Islands

August 19, 1971

Today one of the bats gave birth to a giant baby and I am convinced that were I to discover the reason and rhyme of this extraordinary bat birth I would find something of the trail that life here produces on these magical islands, and thus give some insight into the possibilities for their longevity, as it were.

How big should any *Megaerops ecaudatus* infant be, if indeed a *Megaerops ecaudatus* this infant is?

I have not ever experienced a delivery of this size in all my years. Therefore, forgive me if I am prone to speculation. But I cannot imagine in any bat genus or for any bat reason why an infant would emerge this large into the world, so fully formed or so uncommonly voracious. Or then, for that matter, for an infant to be so ordinarily received by its peers. Because these bats here in the north of these Communion Islands do not for a minute look perplexed or concerned by this enormous arrival. Nor by the considerable mismatch between the infant pup's "baby" size and the so-called "adult" size of its mother, who cannot be any more than eight or ten inches in length herself. And aged.

Yes, remarkably, the mother of this neonate is, by my estimation, six score years, or more, in bat years. A small, hunched and overly furry creature, she is, whose one good shoulder rises and falls with her small flights while her other hangs forward and rolls awkwardly around her tiny fragile axis. She is years older than I am, by Jove!

In the very best conditions she moves slowly. In the worst she stops still and slumps there against a wall, hangs by one claw from the ceiling, or rolls up to stone or piece of driftwood as long as necessity insists. Then she attempts to make her way again, no flight further ahead of her than the one before, a weak heaving movement of airborne activity that belies the conditions under which I find her.

Apparently she has flown along the Communions coast from a point two dozen or so miles hence. Another colony entirely, you'd think; perhaps an entirely different genus. But my reluctant local guides, who seem to view me as Schwartz does as some kind of clawed pariah, indicate that here in these islands there is not the division of colonies of this kind that defines the usual bat social congregations and movements. The gatherings of these bats into what we ostensibly would label "families" or "groups" are not referred to in quite the same way as we would refer to them, being merely recorded in the local dialect as *caocochi*, meaning those places where the inhabitants sometimes congregate, and different thus from *dancochi*, where these bat populations move through on their way elsewhere.

They all come for the abundant fruits, no doubt!

As there is no zonal life, no separate cave or canopy or general tree life as such, little can be done to apply standard analytical reasoning to their disease free longevity, or to elicit any response from my guides to the question of this bat's particular birthplace, usual habitat, or flight patterns. Locales seem to mean very little to these Communion Islanders; only perceived directions and probable movements.

The best my guides can do is to indicate that this female bat is southern, that is not generally from these northern parts, a known unknown having arrived at some point in a non-definable fruit-seeking past and likely to be departing at some time in a non-approachable fruitless future. Such seems to be their way of thinking, perhaps determined by their own history of "disease and despair", as they tend to refer to it.

For her part, the female seems unconcerned by her whereabouts, by my presence or by the presence of the other islanders, for that matter, and takes to the task of feeding her monstrous newborn with such gusto that her small orange frame appears to actually expand in size and then to contract with the rhythm of the infant's suckling. During which, all the time, she lets out a sound akin to the maundering of donkeys or the maaing of goats. She closes her tiny black eyes, collapsed back against the cushion of a mud bank or a sand dune intruding on the cave, and she leaves things to run their course.

I cannot help but ponder the logistics of her neonate's birth, uneducated as I am in the modern field of bat obstetrics (if such a specific field was possible!), and inexperienced as I still might be with the world of bat midwifery. I nevertheless have a reasonable grasp of orthopedics, not to mention a very good understanding of the trigometric conditions of humankind, male or female. I have assisted many times too in areas of muscular or skeletal observation, not least recently in the deterioration of aging tenors, and the association between muscular change and capacity.

In this new *Megaerops ecaudatus* case how one creature has come from another is, truly, a matter of unfathomable disorder. What might have allowed or encouraged such a birth, and in what conditions do such long and healthy lives become ordinary? Indeed, the fact that seems almost impossible to ignore is the creature's age and good health. In human years she would be, by my rough immediate estimation, well over two hundred years of age, yet she is not only healthy and clearly a full and active member of the colony, but she has now given birth to a pup almost six or seven times her size, and done so in a way that suggests her reproductive years are not over.

It strikes me, though I am aware of my own prejudice and my own desires in this regard, that from this extraordinary live birth size might come some indication of the shape of these bats' lives, and from this lived *chiroptera* shape something of the order and attitude of those fruit bat lives as they relate to the possibility for longevity in the human population on these islands.

In the historical past - possibly due to the tissue impact and trauma of this period—the population here foundered in their early adulthood, with a large proportion even succumbing, tragically, in peripuberty and earlier. But it is my contention, that the chances of survival might well be enhanced by the further taking and examination of samples from the islands' prolific and widespread fruit bat population—such that a thing might be revealed about the start and finish of an existence, the habits and the foundations of health and longevity. This is almost impossible imagine at this point, though all indications are that discoveries are now reasonably close at hand.

Here in this birth might well lie a most significant clue, because it makes some sense that an infant of such height and girth can be born without fanfare and without fear only where the capacity to do is enhanced by the ordinariness of what we would call a life lived in the "extraordinary".

In this fact perhaps lies the essence of our capacity to alter the path of human lives here, from one where life is short and founded on such plodding labor against the past to one where robustness and extent are not extraordinary at all. From there the intransitive nature of what we might well provide for the population here becomes clear. It is with that point that any scientist would wish to locate his most vigilant thoughts and, by my clear indication, their erstwhile actions.

Suffice, the old bat is small, even at the wing, but the pup, the new born, is large, even at its fruit seeking mouth. Accurately, the infant must be a good fourteen or eighteen inches in length, stretched out, and at least six or eight inches round, at the center of its abdomen. When I ask the inhabitants, as best as I can, if they have any knowledge of other bat births such as this one, they look at me as though I have spoken so naively, so innocently, that they can't bear to listen to my question, never mind answer it. They wave me away, as I attempt to press them for more.

Some, though covering their mouths and feigning urgent attention to some sea-born thing of considerable importance elsewhere, a fishing net or school of dolphins or a sinking ship or such, actually seem to be breaking into peals of conversation rabid with concern and contention. They scurry off in the direction of their impromptu town gathering concerned, the more forthcoming intimate, with the rising wind that is now turning up its force on cue to cover their pealing tracks and whip the harbor into a bobbling frenzy.

A monstrous eager bat pup, born without fanfare or fuss. Dangerously large by any modern account of *Pteropus conspicillatus* or *Acerodon jubatus* or even *Nyctimene cyclotis*. Born to a bat mother *supposedly* at least three times pup-bearing age, without any obvious indication of strength body or character or condition that might indicate some unique characteristic, solely associated with herself. Other than her age, that is, whose indication is that while she may not be young she is somehow, in ontogenically definitive ways, not all old.

This impossible mix is a beginning of something, some questions if not yet answerable, and if from this grows more evidence and more opportunity for observation, then so be it. As I watch the bat mother now, the giant infant somehow draped across the inside of her rolled rubbery wing, she follows the others with her head, overcoming the gargantuan weight she now bears beyond herself rather than once, as the bat infant must have been, within her. To say there are clues here would be profoundly understating my feelings, and that the bats of this island, of which I yet know so very little, holds them. This seems to me an entirely valid, and exciting, contention.

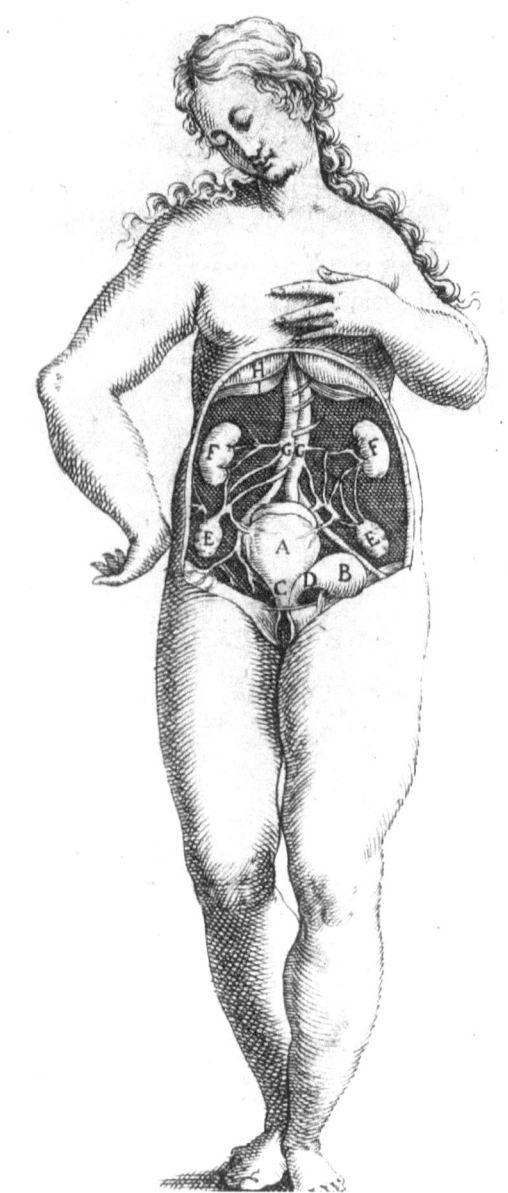

Figure 17.

Our Story

"How came I here?" the portrait thus might speak,
The crimson mantling in its canvas cheek,
"Here in this concourse of the wise and grave
Who look upon me with inquiring eyes,
As on some homeless wanderer, caught astray?"

—Oliver Wendell Holmes
Lines on the presentation of his portrait to the Philadelphia
College of Physicians, April 30th 1892

Still in Search

1.

Exhausted, Death slumped. She slumped in my plane, like half a sack of sweet potatoes slung against the aft door, in and out of sleep. Muttering now and then, indecipherably, her red hat over her eyes and her hands clutching her black battered bag. I did not know what was going through her mind, but I had in my own mind the Communion Islands Community Hospital, which had just opened its doors, and the patients there, and the sight of Panapoon harbor in the late afternoon, as you rise up over it in a small craft, aircraft that is, and turn to the north, with the main street below, all abustle and abright with life, and the colors of the parks, where tourists wander on verdant green with vehement gold ahead of them and imagine—or so I always imagine—that down on our beaches they will find fur seals and beached whales and parts of galleons, a prow or a captain or such, and the jaws of a monstrous shark, and doubloons scattered, and palm trees with their coconut offerings, and turtles laying their neighborhoods of eggs, and lapping shores lapping, lapping, lapping, and their life's one love, and all manner of memories.

2.

Back at the hospital the clerk was in the garden, or among the children inside, or more likely he had taken himself up onto the roof of the hospital and was there on the roof walk, leaning over the slatted railing and looking out toward Scoop Point, or the rocky outcrops of Skelton, or the distant peaks of Cloud Mountain, suitably behind a small icing of cloud, or the main street where hopeful sweepers swept at the sidewalks in rhythmic yet free actions.

That he was barely a third of her age had driven a wedge between some of us—if I can mix this up this way, and leave it stuck up there, jutting from the doorway of it all. I mean, there had been feelings, and from feelings there had been actions. It was a long time, for example (see how I can use the formal tone where it best suits?), for example, before the Apples would visit the clinic again, Penny herself going back to the orchard where, in time she found a new direction, and now tends the front counter for Beninni where you can, indeed, get a lobster in the brown sauce of sea grass, or pick up a handful of shrimp on a bed of shredded local lettuce. It is not that I dislike Beninni as much as it seems, but it has to be said that he was one of those who abandoned both the clerk and his new found love. That he, who had himself come to the Communions when he was barely in his teens and lived on the boats, hunting sailfish and sailing hunters out in search of shark or other more make-believe monsters, catching shrimp and canning tuna, that he was one who should have supported the good doctor. He did not. He railed against her idea for a hospital—at town meetings and so forth. But he was not the only one; and, despite his lack of culinary talent, perhaps I shouldn't dwell.

3.

They fell in love over an idea, the clerk and Death. No more and no less. From that love they transformed a past into a future, or thereabouts. We still have to deal with the general, destructive frailty of human beings, of course. Worse things have happened; but, in this case, few better ones.

Awaking from their stuporous meeting, their memories of the night before little more than a blur of lights and glass, an unfathomable encounter with a banana tree, the sounding of a ship's horn, a fall on the grass, a rise along a blue painted harbor railing, a mouthful of sand, cold on the bare feet, the smell of a night fire on the main beach, Captain Horton's Island Rum. You say no good things come of drunkenness? Have you ever read Mahinima, Petersen or Corbett, or the Communion Islands Almanac? Have you never seen happiness unearthed from the sodden black soil of a bog, heaved up onto the side of that moldy lake and cracked open sparkling with a claw hammer?

Then you have seen the love of young clerk and not so young Death. She was a good thirty years his senior, but what did it matter? If you have crossed a coal pit, or crawled out of a sack of sticking pears, if you have thought about the hard rush of the sea when a winter tide turns and the inner whirl of the sea wall no longer houses the smallest silvery fish but churns and thrusts at the rock as if might overturn it and you and the entire town then . . .

Well, I wildly lyricize again, and I do apologize!

But they caught each other, then, when she was in the clutches of some aged operatic fool, and he was in the drift of the idea that he belonged neither in the mountains of his family nor to the beaches of his ambition. He'd have left the islands if not for her, I'm sure of it. And she'd have never truly discovered them. They collided, and if Fate was responsible then to Fate I take off my aviator's bonnet and swing it leatherly around my head. They collided, but not in that way that breaks apart some contraption or ruins a good horse, but in that way of two sandbars coming together in a current, and shifting and smoothing around each other, each grain slipping against another, every direction explored all at once, until the direction of one and of the other is no longer discernibly different, and the crazy dance of their meeting seems to have generated something else entirely, the water beyond no longer dictating anything.

4.

Watching her sleep there as we flew over the Burdekin and then the Ackeronites, across the banana plantations just south, with their neat wide leafy rows dipping along the hefty rich ridges, down then over the lower Yool hills, to the east of already twinkling Monkthorton, and then the sight of Skelton, or the yellow lights there against the sea at least, with the sun beginning to go down behind and to the right of us - she seemed to have gained something and lost an entire half her weight.

Death was curled now almost fully in the seat and the thought I had previously that she was her full self was no longer even remotely believable. The evening shadows gave it away, catching the unfilled contours of her there. She was half of what she was, the long brown weave of her sweater huge over her arm, her shoulders, her dress beneath, something I believe is referred to as "a smock", lay like some yards of newspaper, stiff with the Anka, its mud, its saltwater and its heat. But stiff it was, because nothing was holding it out there. Paper thin she had become. She had literally disappeared into her journey, and whatever she had found up there, whatever reasons the bat-loving doctor had for staying away these months, what that was she was bringing it back. That was her replacement. Her new self. Her old self had been left behind.

THE
Cure of Old Age,
AND
Preservation of Youth.

By *ROGER BACON*,

A Francifcan Frier.

Tranflated out of Latin; with Annotations, and an Account of his Life and Writings.

By *Richard Browne*, M. L. Coll. Med. Lond.

ALSO
A Phyfical Account
OF THE
Tree of Life,
BY
EDW. MADEIRA ARRAIS.

Tranflated likewife out of Latin by the fame Hand.

LONDON,

Printed for *Tho. Flesher* at the *Angel* and *Crown*, and *Edward Evets* at the *Green Dragon*, in Sᵗ *Pauls* Church-yard.   168₃.

Figure 18.

Death's Story

Who lives in death, by death in death is lying;
But he who living dies, best lives by dying:
Who life to truth, who death to errour gives,
In life may die, by death more surely lives.

—*P. Fletcher*
The Purple Island, Or The Isle of Man Together with Piscatorie
Eclogs and other Poeticall Miscellanies, 1633.

Firstly, At the Beginning

1.

It came down to a matter of truth and of will and of true intention and, ultimately, survival. The truth was - and as anyone could see my intentions were already entirely clear and my heart already stolen, that the tenor, for all this tremendous rills and smooth intonation, his booming fortissimo and his want of muscle—the tenor was no longer being profoundo when it came to paying his bills. I could not go back, I could not leave The Communion Islands, even if I wanted to, bats or no bats. As to the previous young man, whose love was no more or less than this new one, but less honest, I have to say, and perhaps less ardent, I had not deceived him. The previous magistrate had erred. My reputation stood on its plinth, carved and etched and unsullied.

These things duly considered—and I use the word "duly" here in recognition of the import that arriving in The Communions Islands had brought upon me, and the possibilities it held. I had been many places, for research, for bat search, for the belief that somewhere in the world I would find my true place and there, truthfully placed, make a difference. To someone, and to me! I had gone to medical school with this very intention. We all had - except for the surgeons, mostly, that was, whose meaning was more financial and less communicative. Even that denigrates their species. Some were bolder and wiser and more human that others. We junior surgeons, ophthalmologists, hematologists, gynecologists, endocrinologists, cardiologists, neurologists: we all had our ways!

Regardless, I was committed to my route, and I replied to the Clerk of the Communion Islands Government Offices, which at that point may just have as well been an invention for all I knew (entrance, second in the row beside a magic cave or in the bowels of a fantasy castle) confirming my clear conscience, and I arrived via seaplane at the clerkdown the following Monday with my bag and my life and my thoughts of the future.

"Here on The Communion Islands," I thought, "where the past has been short of years and long of hardship, I will discover more than the mere maintenance of humankind, and partake (even pursue!) their actual, subsequent advance."

"It is the 1970s," I told myself, "after all! We can put a man on The Moon, we should be able to sustain a population on earth, for goodness sake!"

2.

The building housing the Communion Islands Government Offices was, naturally enough and for recognizable reason, an imposing building. It had three faces of marble, no doubt hewn from the bogs and trenches of that jungle around Cuuk and beyond the hard coal country that the elder of the population here calls "The Vent", referring I think to the fervent that created the islands in the first place, island upon island, staring over their inky passages and turquoise reefs, toward each other.

There were Italianate pillars as thick as four men—to hold up its stories, incidentally, not for the sheer hewn arrogance—bright and clean and white, and a caretaker's quarters or two, and garages and boatsheds, at the rear, all in most uneventful brown wood. It was a building three times the height of all others, even that string of urgent seaside hotels, which reminded me of hotels everywhere in their floral lobbies and their uniformed attendants, their careful placement of picture and post, so that where you might seek a spittoon one would miraculously appear and where you might stumble on an un-inviting vista, a palm would *surreptitiously* wave its shiny ver-dancy across your otherwise clear sight, to block it out.

Being at the peak of a rise, the rising clip of the Panapoon escarpment, those island government buildings took the full height of that rich red Communions earth and sandy rock and philfond trees into its decidedly governmental stratum and looked down over Panapoon Harbor and the Pleasant River with all the majesty of a temple and the imposition of the brand new horizon.

All this you would never know, however, had you not been introduced to it, because you reached the building along a narrow drive, between the Coppersmith Hotel and Gnatville Café, or something like that—no great joint, that's for sure. A wondrous disguise and one which, right from the start, did not escape me!

For The Communion Islands, which is young even now, the Offices' history was apparently surprisingly long, like the thick snake of a mooring rope that slung itself into the har-bor and out beyond the headlands, back through island time. It took into its operational realm, which covered the entire Communion Islands from Shelton Beach to Yool, from Cop-ple to Sea Ridge, Petersville to Fenton, Welson to Welson Mountain, all the operations of islands.

Though the permanent "front of house" staff was just two, a young girl called Apple being the second of these I soon dis-covered, it was home to a constant itinerant bunch of island petitioners and providers, local workers and island deliverers, a seaplane pilot, a boat captain or two or three in their rubberized pants and checked shirts, a weekly supply of inquirers, complainers and wonderers, who came into the Offices and disappeared somewhere inside, in search of substance, in search of reason, in search of themselves maybe, and left some time later, bearing accomplishment, or something like that.

Yet, imposing though they were, it was obvious to me that the Offices' most miraculous feature were their inappropriateness.

On an islands so absent of long life, so threateningly *sans* good medical care, with a history of despair and a population of local children who knew no other than the probability of disease and the impossibility of medicine itself, modern or otherwise, the Offices seemed to me out of keeping and, in that way, strangely isolated, despite their location, removed from Communion Islands life.

It felt like some creature from beyond the mighty Moon and hot-hearted Mars had descended, in the past, and deposited them there—five metaphoric leagues from the nearest real person, and marked them with a black stone tablet by a tall iron gate. The Offices had stood like that, through the years, with their clerk and their visitors heading on inward to who knows what or where, since the hotels were built in front of them and the new pavement was laid along the Play Park (the same day, if the scrawled notice on the nearby hotel wall was correct, that the famous Christian Barnard washed his brilliant hands in the African waters and, with sweet Ethanol then in the air, went out to perform a feat of human engineering so miraculous as to challenge understanding, or emotion at least)

Into that mystery of a building I entered, with my best embroidered kufi in my hand, and enquired at the Reception desk for the whereabouts of the Clerk.

"Absent," replied the girl on the desk, who wore a nice green top, I noticed, and a fancy frock (it best be called) of crimson linen.

This was a young woman, I thought, who preserved herself for other things—possibly reading the turns in the local weather or walking along the harbor front with her beast beau.

"Indeed," I said, with a show of teeth, in hope of matching my reply to the slap of her shoe's heels on the hard wooden floor.

The girl made her green top jiggle like she was holding back and earthquake and told me Mr S__ was unavailable until 9.00 am. To be accurate, this was not true.

These Young Islands

1.

The fact was, Samuel (as soon I'd know him and he, not to put too fine a point on it, would soon knowingly know with me) had risen before dawn—dawn rises in the Communions like a slatted cane blind pulled up abruptly—in the hope of catching the bigger Gorbbi fish, which lie in wait for the thousands of fingerlings of green fish, in the shallows on the beach below the Offices, when the Moon is absent and the nights are Spring warm and the only sounds are the shrill nut beetles and the cunning feral rustlings of, I suppose, escaped ships' cats.

It annoyed his largely youthful self when he rose (from his island bed made up of a weed thin striped mattress and not much else because of his upper peninsula heritage) that the clouds of the night before hadn't drifted away, as he thought they might, nor shed their light load over the coastal plain, feeding parambolas and tree figs, and then turned white on the mountains behind. He expressed himself like this:

"Sometimes I hate the sky. Are you listening up there?! Sometimes . . . "

And rolled about on the weed mattress a moment until something turned sweeter inside him, propelled him up and pressed his face to the window of his room.

He knew the clouds continuing meant that the sunrise proper, which should have come by now, would not come until later; and, by then, the Gorbbi would have moved on to the deeper water, up stream, where they would change their tactics. He could not expect to catch one Gorbbi with his preparations for another. He'd need to thread new line through his runners—literally, though this also has poignant metaphoric meaning—and change his hooks to short silver barbs from the long shanked brown hooks he used on the shallows.

"Cah, cah cah," he said (or sung, more accurately) as he changed his rigging. This, he thought, would now be the fishing of tourists and nothing to do and inattention and ignorance. All these things, and those words, went through his handsome head.

By the time the sun proper had bobbed up over the boat sheds and cottages of the government Offices Samuel already had his line strung into the channel from a rig that is known locally in The Communion Islands as a "Swift Cast". You can see him there, in the vision of time, with his glistening line taut in the water, right there at the turn of tide, moving neither up nor down. His index finger, observably long at the proximal phalanx, and calloused even then, acts like an elegant clockwork lever, cranking the line lightly up and lowering it lightly down, simulating life! A magnificent creature, reminiscent of a lion seal, there on the water's edge.

Yes, "life, life, life" he was singing. Jig, jig jig.

With his eyes fixed on the water, staring now at a point exactly between his finger and what civilized man has come to call "infinity" but which is, in reality, something far more interesting. There, staring, he dispensed with everything else. The world might as well have been a figment at that moment, a wisp on a leaf or the curl of dust he could see when the sun charges an ion over a road's edge.

After a while, in what I came to know was his predictable success, the line snapped taught.

He let out a small sound: "Tuuuuuuuuuwwww. . . ."

Then he let the biter run. I have not seen this in many men, though I recall one neurosurgeon, who worked in the rooms around Golders and the greener parts of London, who claimed that an entire tribe of Chinese folk had the ability to control their involuntary nervous system so that even a sneeze could be stopped mid-flight. Samuel let the fish sweep eagerly toward deeper water, turning outward as wide as it liked.

"As wide as a dozen old dead men," he told me, though I suspect this was just to catch a moment of my clinical interest.

Swerving northward, into the main channel that runs between the Pleasant River and the Panapoon beach. Then . . .

Hauling, hauling against the tug of the fish. In silhouette, he looked like a harp player - I can just about hear his delicate notes—then, the next moment, like a horseman preparing the white tail of an Arabian. Then - touché! - like an avid traveler tossing gold coin after coin into an ancient burbling fountain as it burbles up for him.

He tugged in steady rises and falls of his rig.

2.

You see how neither love nor medicine are matters of simplicity? The same can be said of fruit bats - if you can might bear with me a batty moment.

A fruit bat is a creature made of many parts, none of which belong with the other. You'll have noticed the foxified snouts of the creatures, if the sub-genus is not the Tube-nose, that is, whose snout is as you can well imagine, and, of course, then there's the Tailless, and the Dusky, and the Lesser, and the Harpy, and the Long-Tongued, and the White-Winged and the . . . There are, at last count, over five dozen discovered genus, and several well-populated sub-families. Not to labor the point, though the comparison I'm making will have grown already to clear dimensions by now. No, the fruit bat is never simple or similar, never found by its clear indications or lost by the imagination.

Now imagine medicine, and love. Imagine Samuel at work with his fish, an inwardly young man with wayfaring heart but island loving ways. Imagine Barnard at work with his scalpel, boldly. Imagine a ship, its sails full of a stiff Communion Islands easterly, on the reach of the north coast where the shores are barely broken, jungles and outcrops and the like, its decks all awash, a wiry red bearded captain at the wheelhouse, a dozen laboring crew at the ropes, children below decks wheezing and fevering. Imagine finding an avenue where blossoms fall to the pavement in more than one color, all year 'round.

When I was in my freshmen biochemistry class an old biochemist, name of Constable, hailing from one of those ancient English towns by the name of Westchester, or Wandleton, Chestertontown or somewhere like that, told me that as a student he had once fallen entirely and uncontrollable in love with *monosaccharides*, on account of their perfectly equal joining of one molecule of sugar and one of carbon.

Medicine is controlled love of the probable, with a mix of the impossible. I was thinking about how Barnard had done it: with his scalpel and adventurousness, to translate an entire heart.

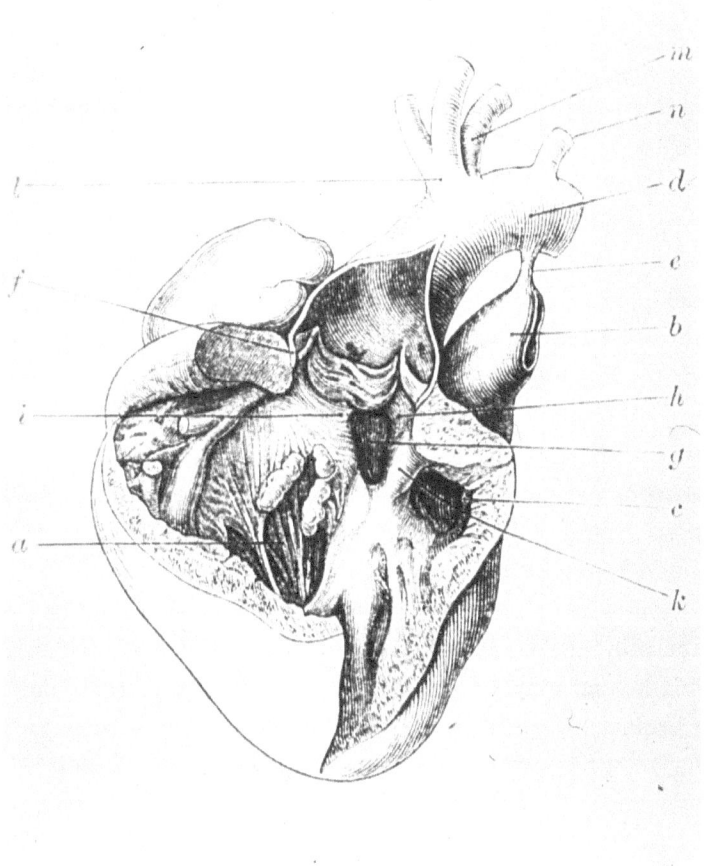

Figure 19.

In time - and to cut a long story short—my future Samuel drew the Gorbbi into the lolling waters of the inner bank below Panapoon Beach.

"Made for this," he said, reveling in the line strain, referring to the rig as it swung and tore in the water. His hands were twitching and there was a numbness which he also felt, but ignored. There in the now later morning shallows, the fish threshed and fought more vigorously, with its big silver tail slicing at the warm Communions air, for all the world some kind of miniature shark, though the Gorbbi are mostly a creature of the upper or back waters, spawned in small mountain streams beyond Coppel and Upper Yool. It popped its bull head up and blackly eyed its captor. Its big mouth gaped. If it could have spoken. . . .

But it came up, flipping, on that there Samuel fish line (to abuse an apparent local dialect). And he rested it on a flat rock just behind him, on the week before's Communion Island's *Chronicle*, moistened. He turned the barbed hook in its gaping mouth—two spots of blood diligently jumped onto the newspaper (just above the headline, I like to think, though I have no evidence)—and he began measuring that fish with the span of his hand.

One, two, three: his hands speaking like this. Its fins continued swimming beneath his fingers, brushing back and forth, its eyes circulated ring within ring.

"What was that Gorbbi's eye filled with?" I wonder.

Fear, you'd expect.

"Hope," Samuel told me later.

A lifelong fisherman, he said: "People think a caught fish feels fear, but how can it, don't you know, when it has nothing to compare with? What he feels," he said, sitting with a line stringing from the jetty behind the boatshed, "is hope. You know, hope that things will make sense in a minute. Hope. Hope that whatever is going on will be good."

Hope then. An eye filled with the substance of hope. Hope overtaking hope until perhaps what that Gorbbi's eye became was a reflection of hope in general (or, so I like to think, as I hovered there beyond the scene, awaiting my time in the Communions).

And Samuel, thinking of getting to his clerk's desk, unhappy with the cloud, but the day now beginning to grow brighter, joking away with himself, hopefully:

"When is a fish not a fish?"

The joking clerk.

"When it's aflounder-ing."

But strangely, you could say, or not so, something was going on. Not the bicycling sounds of cooks and cleaners on their way to work at the seafront of hostels, and not the fishermen on their boats, coming into the rocky lips of the harbor, to coin a sweet phrase, and not the sound of the world's adventurers emerging from the hostels and spouting their innocent wandering somethings at the emerging Communions sun, but the joining of the clerk world and the fish world. Some strange impossibility that had it not been true could not have happened.

He could feel the hope himself now, familiar as it was, in his very own belly. It overcame him, suddenly; brought together his aging exterior with his perpetually youthful interior. And he pulled himself back from it, his hard boot on the Gorbbi. It might have been at that moment that Samuel and I fell in love, though we had not then yet met. But hope of that kind, mixed with ambition and confusion, is a force to be reckoned with, and though we did not know each other, did not even know what we would one day meet, could not even contemplate a meeting between the inner workings of The Communion Islands and the outer arrival of a foreign doctor, it might well have been at that moment that we fell for each other. The next time his hands clasped the fish, they did so no less gingerly. But he took that staring fish, left hand under its pulsing gills and right hand behind its springing dorsal fin and, with one huge shouldered movement, flung the fish into the deep dark channel.

Figure 20.

Outgoing Mail

1.

Somewhere else entirely, and to provide here a jovial inter-
lude of the colorful kind you find in "true adventure" stories,
novels, and what is known as The Classical Cinema, Miss
Penny Apple, when she awoke that morning, said to the small
hirsute gentleman lying prostrate and, not to put too fine a
point on it, prone beside her:

"Yes, yes, do you know: I hear our first official physician is
to be a man with a nose the size of a banana, the feet of a mal-
lard duck, the eyes of a gibbon and a voice like two hundred
miles of broken road?"

The gentleman, who might just as easily hailed from some
outer island of Loon-Over-Loon, or thereabouts anyway, but
was actually from much further afield (in space and time, incidentally!), hadn't known Miss Apple longer than it took to
moor his boat (so to speak), bulged out his already bulging
grey eyes, hoiked up his truss, adjusted his withered old leg
in the sagging sack of a sack, and contemplated the descrip-
tion—which Miss Apple then quickly laughed off, jumping
from the bed with a "Well, so says Trevor Felmore!", referring
to the conversation that had so filled the Panapoon Post Office
the previous morning that there was no room for anyone else.

"Our first resident physician is a very well-respected doctor,
do you know?" Mr Felmore had said, to the street cleaners

who were in there sipping their morning teas. "He belongs to a well-known family of London doctors, but has no living relatives, other than a brother, I hear."

"Does he come experienced?" asked Erinyes, the chief cleaner, whose head bore an uncanny resemblance to an enlarged Communion Islands fig.

"Of many many years," piped up Kitty Felmore, from behind her husband but to the right, encapsulating a bamboo frond and a rice paper room divider featuring a white ibis. "My word she does."

"And with a famous family, do you know?

"Drs Thompson. A fine, fine reputation," continues Kitty.

(I think you can hear their child-like voices in the wind as they converse).

"Do you think this Thompson will mind the others who have been doing his job?" asked Tippy Cryer.

"Others, Tip Cryer?" asked Penny, entering the Post Office with a skip and a jump reminiscent of one of those jodhpurred horse women who harass innocent visitors at the Panapoon Derby and the Something Something grand Something Grand National. "No one need ask who you mean?"

Penny Apple considers the party of cleaners as if they are black gulls soaring back and forth above her sheets on the washing line.

"Others?" echoed Trevor, who liked a drink after dark in the quiet iron chamber of the open Post Office safe.

"I was merely saying that Sam S__ has advised and inspected," continued the atonal Ms Cryer, "whether there was a rhyme or reason to his diagnoses I cannot say, do you know. I merely suggest that it might be nice if we all were not so dependent any longer on . . . chance."

"Tippy," cried Penny, clasping her small round waist as if about to shoot for a basket, "the new doctor is a monster, and a lecherer. So whether we need this man at all is another matter.

(To tell the truth she did not say this, but I feel the need to insert my own interpretation, given the impact my arrival will have on island history, otherwise all I can report is a pregnant silence and the sight of two brown dogs wandering shoulder against shoulder along the sea front, sniffing the breeze. There were more things than that at stake).

"Not for the want of doctors here, do you know," said Kitty (or so I insert).

"No," said Trevor insertingly, "not for the want."

Had they known it was the good Dr Thompson in Penny Apple's bed, who knows what might have occurred!

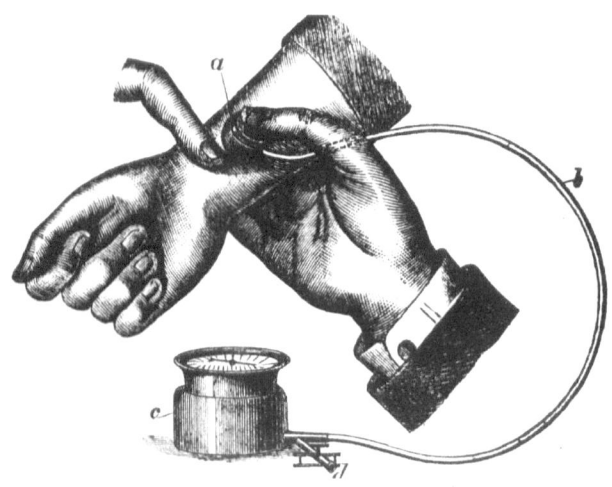

Figure 21.

2.

There is a short story someone could tell here. *Viva debate*, perhaps! *Viva narrative!* A story about visiting doctors to The Communion Islands, of which Dr Thompson, so called, was an example.

There had been doctors. There had been many doctor visitors, in fact. They had come on ships and stayed in hostels. They had flown in seaplanes and arrived in the dripping caverns of jolly cruise ships. They had visited in times of trouble and sometimes caused trouble in quieter times. They were carriers of black bags and wearers of white coats. They had come, but they had left.

They had left, and things continued without them.

There were suggestions, at times, and borne on the back of a history of island disease and a penchant for local elaboration, that the islands should have their own medical rooms, rather than boating and flying island folks to the nearby mainland of __where the elements of foreign exchange and the intentions of foreign governments gave no guarantee of medical success. But the Communions were not far enough, and the Communions were not wealthy enough, and the Communions had not the independence enough, to found their own institutional dynasty. So the story goes.

You could insert here several characters and have perhaps heard the stories of the period of early deaths, life expectancies which were not expectant at all, quarantine ships, a flushing of viral contact from the islands so that visitors now came entirely inoculated and islanders inoculated against them. What doctors there had been the population tended to unremember—which is different from forgetting, in that there remained a dark shadow of visiting physicians, a silhouette of emergency surgeons, research virologists, traveling quacks.

By which I mean, the small island population was aware that they had survived these past two hundred years on the back of visitors but they had grown up beyond this, despite their childlike qualities.

3.

"Not for want of wanting," continued Trevor Phelmore, brilliantly franking a parcel and counting out a handful of change from one of his wooden drawers into another. "But this new man, Thompson, plans to lodge here, and make Panapoon his home."

(I had not agreed to anything, but being as they were not talking about me anyway. . .)

"And to train his assistants in the British manner."

(Nothing had been said).

"And he plans to build a new islander from the remnants of the old", he might as well have added.

(Dr Frankenstein, I presume).

The seagulls each opened their mouths in unison and would probably have sung a cawing song for the incoming doctor, if not that their tea was gone and their brooms awaited.

"And they say," said Penny, as she headed back out the door, and with a hint that maybe she knew exactly what she was doing, "that he sometimes doctors naked in the summer. You know, with the heat and everything."

"Naked," she said, grinning out the door, "completely, he is."

But maybe I insert, maybe I insert, maybe I insert too much.

And Now a Doctor for The Communion Islands

Let me draw you a picture of Penny Apple's island visitor, the lost Dr Thompson, newly arrived but not where he was supposed to be. Let me sketch him as he accurately appears in his sweeping vista and his swept victories.

I take up my sharpened pencil, thus. I inspect my parchment, thus: ostensibly clean and textured white, quite naturally. I stand out on the red ridge above the surging Spook Reef, with the beaut brewt forests of Store Cove to the left and the little brown fishermen's cottages of Yawl yawling to the right. And I begin thus, and thus:

He is peculiar. His hair, which is peculiarly thick for his peculiar age, seems to contain too much starch, peculiarly. He is the collar prepared for a military man's shirt, or the proud pleat in the trouser of a circus ringmaster. He scrubs until his skin is springing. In fact, it looks as though it might spring right off and stand there, skin and visitor separate.

Outside, with this grey ridge of rock thatch, his shale fin, firm in the breeze, he circles her old yellow sedan, eyeing it brutally.

"How's she go?" he says, for no apparent reason.

And: "Yes, yes, yes, yes."

He clothes are unfathomable shiny, a kind of tin foil armor I suspect, though they have hung over the rail of Penny's small white harbor cottage all night like flags warning sailors of an approaching easterly squall:

"I am changing my course to starboard" or:

"I am on fire and have dangerous cargo. Keep clear".

Might I speculate? Thusly:

Here is the kind of gent who abhors rust, but likes the islands for their rusty tones. Here is the kind who knows the models of cruising craft but prefers not to spend too much time at sea, as it weakens "his resolve". Here is the kind that likes detergents and sprays, the scents and the results. He is the kind that drinks in saloon bars, but only the sort in which he appears out of place, where the conversation is about things in which he has no experience, and no genuine interest, loggers' bars, and fishermen's' bars and the bars of miners and mechanics and drivers and divers. Here is a gent, even Penny might have thought, who buys everyone a drink, but seems not to know why. He sleeps in his socks, shiny as stars as they are. Maybe - though she does not dare think it—he has some partial denture, the top hung there so obtrusively, cemented as firmly as possible to the roof of his deep mouth perhaps. His back is covered a sparse forest of black pine hairs. Sometimes she wonders where his knees have gone, because they seem to be there one moment and gone the next, as he rolls forward.

"Elusive," she told him, when he asked about his best qualities.

"You are elusive."

And he roared with a kind of laughter that may have been genuine or may have been the product of cogs and wheels, a greasy piston engine, a length of rubbery track, oil, gas and chains, turbines and nuts and bolts.

"I'll take you," she said to him.

He made all kind of significant declarations as she drove him to the bus station, the first being that he was a man of his word and would not merely return to his own glittering, sky-scraped world but would be right back.

"In May," he said, surveying the twittering flocks of November on the sandy shore.

He told her she was a beauty. He spoke as if he was conducting the entire orchestra of a vast Eastern European country.

"Like an angel," he batoned, as her small yellow car revved up the rise.

Up with the oboes, expressivo for the violins, continue you piccolos!

"I have never seen such a creature," he capriccioed.

The timpanis rumbled along the ocean front as two large banana trucks pulled out from the entrance to the harbor, as she skipped up the outer lane, avoiding the turn to the fish factory and swinging around the pole of the green harbor light that blinked softly in the morning sun.

"You mark my word," he said.

And marking it she was.

By the time she was pulling her car into the dusty bay beside the buses, idling, she was imagining him humping a mountain gorilla. Or so I insert. At least, she was imagining his trip to Cuuk would see him gone, and she looked at him as one might look at the slowly ebbing turquoise tide over pocked mud flats or at base of the Cloud mountains when the peaks are all but covered in wisps of cloud. She leaned an inch or two and bit the corner of his mouth when she kissed him, and conducting himself out the door in the direction of the now loading bus, he was gone.

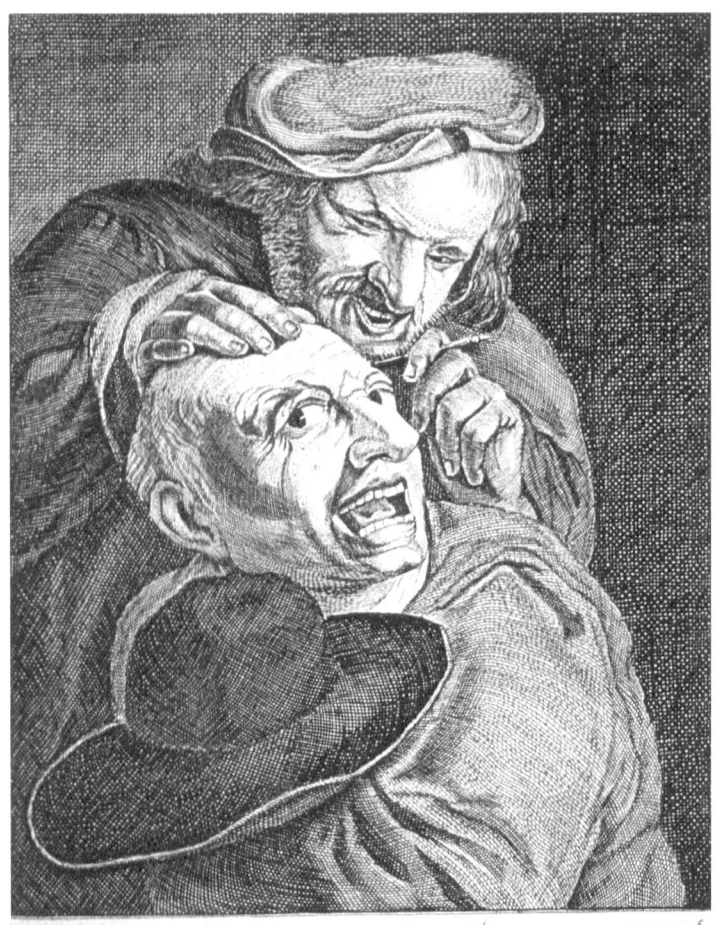

FEELING

Feeling of E'ry Sense the Best
is thus indeed the most distrest
Wo! man 'tis hell it self to Feel
instead of Girl, the Surgeons Steel.

Figure 22.

Me: Alternatively

1.

Samuel, bless his islander innocence and good willing, arrived back at his rooms just before that moment when Penny Apple began jigging up the reedy roller shutter to the Offices, and settling on a tall stool behind the counter. Imagine an ibis, a stork, a crane, and you have there: Penny. So that she might greet visitors who enter looking for fisheries, or aviaries, or the inner workings of the planet around the point of The Communion Islands, where the core is thin and the weather warm. Or something like that!

But there is Samuel, in a delightful mockery of the silliness, simply going about his business, like that famous minstrel in that famous novel, *The Wandering Minstrel*. Quite a minstrel he was!

In Samuel's room the telephone was ringing. He took it with fish catching hands, saying neatly, mouth momentarily gaping:

"Sweet"

Sweet of Sweet's, son of his mountaineering father and croc wrestling mother. Well, she raised five children, at very least, and helped build their mountain house, which was no small feat, given its place "on the hill' as they call it in the Communions, and being made of local stone, hewn and captured and daubed by hand. Cliffs to one side and the jagged blackwood forests of the Upper Cuuk to the other. Raised her kids on the cliffs, and kept them alive, made jams, toasted birds, spun entire winters out of two wild goats and the hair of a stout legged and moping old horse. That kind of thing! And from that came Samuel and from Samuel came the honesty of his upbringing. These things have their connections.

"Sweet,' he repeated.

And then, from the earpiece of the telephone, boomed the new doctor's voice.

People generally believe a doctor's voice should boom. Beliefs run strong on this, through human history and the like. After all, it is the voice of anatomical authority —so called at least by those medical theoreticians, Smith and Weston (those sons of guns). I know some masculine doctors who can tell a man his leg is his arm, and he'll believe it. Even start walking on his hands and so forth - so the reports go, anyhow. You would think this booming authority would be to the disadvantage of a woman. But all that booming, all that thundering competition - a woman doctor can insert a whisper to good effect, or pin someone's hopes on a length of sweet studied silence.

"There is trouble," the soon to be appointed doctor said, boomingly. If there was more, he was not immediately getting it out.

"Trouble?" inquired Samuel, the cut of his collar stabbing the air beside the telephone.

Jumping ahead, it could just as well be said that the old Estuary doctor was trying to offer his apology, his "sincere and urgent apology", or so he later concocted in some leisurely bar on a leisurely bar stool, chugging down another leisurely shot of leisurely Old Maid. But never being inclined to apologize, I guess, he was having trouble getting it out. That old Bowbell practitioner, long of tooth and short of patience, was telephoning to say the he'd be arriving in the Communions later than scheduled. His wife—Lady Mabel of Sussex or Lady Maureen of Essex or of Suspects, probably—she so loved to cycle. Her arms on the throats of two handlebars, stout legs akimbo, hat strapped on her noggin like a green china dinner plate cemented up there. She'd been riding "on the heath" (some kind of hedge) and, while minding her own business (for once) had had the misfortune to ride right smack into a workman's ditch.

Plop!

"The mindlessness of some people astounds me!" says the doctor.

Not me.

By thrashing around to get out of the mindless trap (instead of shoving her fascinator in the hole left by the root of philfond and hoving her gargantuan frame up the clay side, as she might have done) she had caught her delicate lady sensibility on a length of carelessly laid around rock, and damaged her pride.

Strangely, there was something about the absent doctor's voice that Samuel, my future Samuel that is, found compelling. Perhaps it was the memory of that dear old uncle who, having learnt to climb trees in the upper Communions, later left on a steamship "for the Orient", and returned with an accent resembling pebbles rolling on a small bay beach, and a wife and two dozen offspring to boot.

"I wish her a speedy and successful recovery," replied Samuel.

Thinking the absent, no longer arriving doctor a decent man in a tough spot, he said that he'd sort the matter of his late arrival out, and probably would have done, had not unique circumstances stepped in, brandishing a solution.

Figure 23.

2.

Did it happen like that? I think it did. Did I play a role? I certainly will. Did the world stop a moment as the excuse-making doctor, prostrate over a grand piano, somewhere around Heath's Hedge or Portabello Road no doubt, announced he could not make it for the agreed and contractual date? No, it did not.

The islands still needed a doctor. The doctor still needed to arrive. The situation was still grave. The need was still real. The world still was turning.

I have often wondered, in those quiet moments when a woman's head turns to wild fantasies and that warm glow of consideration overcomes even a rational person, what would have happened if the old bonecutter had made it on time. If I had not stepped in, and taken his place. I can see a great expanse of white porcelain across the entire escapement of Skelton Beach, the reflective shine of bedpans from an enclosed yard beside the harbor. I see nurses in crisp white wandering along Panapoon beach, giggling in conversation, and "The Hospital Brass Band" hauling high their golden tubas in our beachside Green Park. I see men in moustaches with index fingers raised proclaiming: "Pancreas!" and "Spleen!" And all along the roadways, signposts, one after another, after another, pointing toward "Scenic Location". On the fore-lawn of every home there would be a slowing mediating "sprinkler", *woosh . . . woosh . . . woosh,* and in the rear-lawn a prim "clothes hoist". And out along the Cuuk road, between the banana stands and the auto repair shambles, heading out of town, beside the fields of peas and the signs for Pineapple Petes, Nut Picking, Guavas, there would be street lamps, tall and green I suspect, with glowing yellow heads.

When Samuel hung up the telephone—"Click!" There it goes—the twitching that earlier had begun to animate his hands (for reasons of decency, and of love, I did not mention) and numbed his fingers was beginning to jab and loop its way down his long fingers and into the balled muscles of his legs. It headed, unperturbed, unannounced, unknown to anyone except himself, onward to his otherwise firm feet.

He glanced, thus, up—at the telephone number of the absent doctor which he had pinned there, like a beam of sunshine, on the window frame behind his desk and around the window, as you'd expect, overlooking the dusty roadway and, just beyond, past the rears of the hotels and the fronts of the banana trucks, to the glistening water of the bay. Some months earlier (how many months I have never been told), in the rooms of a Dr Joel (son of the famous Monty Joel, perhaps, who invented the inflatable sock—well, useless as either Joel had so then been to him), on the mainland __ he had heard, laboriously, a diagnosis:

"Technically," Joel said, grabbing a word from the shelf of complacency and sending it careening across the mahogany room toward his patient, "technically, the cells (note the language) of your body, have begun to increase the fat deposition in the cytoplasm to an alarming rate."

(Inserting for the native English speaker: cell situation, losing fat, patient in trouble)

"The membranes of your cells are being converted into fibrous tissue."

Meaning that in Samuel's body were emerging thousands of tiny unfilled spaces, a space emerging where previously solid Samuel had been, cell by cell, as if he was a remote island chain of tropical mountains on which were located mountains in which were opening up caves and in those caves each was deepening so that. . . . But maybe I make the connection between Samuel and the Communions and the habitats of bats too closely. Maybe if I say that the __ was saying he was turning into an ancient archipelago is taking things too far. His cells atophosphorizing, as it's called, one island of him at a time. But this is too much! Too *much*!

"The number of cells in a body alters constantly, Mr __," weaved the doctor, in his basketing diagnosis. "The colonies divide and reproduce."

(The mainland doctor divided his legs, and reproduced a walk to his latticed window).

"Though the cells . . . errr, die . . . after a number of doublings, others then come along."

He doubled back on his tracks and stood over Samuel, forthwith.

"Your cells, on the other hand, Mr __, are constant. They are a finite number."

("Much like a collection of tokens earned on a now inoperative carnival rollercoaster," I reply from the future, beyond the pontificating mainland doctor's room, and the quiet and the bright and unyielding light).

"You are made up of the exact same bits you had when you were born. . . . Somewhere in the low billions, to be accurate."

Despite the pedantry of Joel, you get the drift.

That was why Samuel was aging as he was, from the inside out, from the agedness of his interior to the youthfulness of his exterior. Strictly speaking—and I'm not making excuses, incidentally!—he was already beyond my age.

At first, as he explained this to himself in the early evenings, alone, in the front room of the Communion Islands Government Offices, he called this:

"The thing within me."

But as he soon realized, this was hardly the case because, if the truth be stated, this thing was without him. That was the point. He revised, therefore:

"I am whittling me away."

And further, less positively (or truly): "My hollow core."

And still more, or less: "I'm my own murderer."

Sweet, literal Samuel!

He returned to the islands from __ no more (for certain) and yet no less than he had temporarily left it. He was only seventeen, but within he was approaching sixty. His insides were like the tanned skin of a nineteenth century sloop sailor, caught in a current off the coast of the Far East and returned to shore on a length of driftwood a hundred years after he had left it. If not for the courage of his exterior, which held him up and out, he'd already have become unrecognizable to those who, as otherwise was the case, continued to recognize him.

When he shaved in the mornings—because I feel the need to include here a personal observation that might enlighten further—when he shaved, his youthful yet aged nostrils flared like two sides of a naked flame, fighting each other. He had begun to think of himself as both here and gone and to act accordingly.

"You are too late!" he shouted, as people came in through the door of the Offices, first thing in the morning.

"Too late?! You mean too early?"

No, he meant too late. If he was aging inside out, and if he was the son of the mountains where giant philfonds fell, and his mother had raised a dozen children, and the gullies beyond Welson and Morphew and the other small towns contained rivers and those rivers came up from beneath those mountains and those mountains had been made of felsic lava, which emerged from the sea, and still has the slight aroma of salt and potassium which attracts *Pteropodidae*, or the fruit bat.

But enough said!

He felt as if he was becoming the ancient there, in person! On his right leg two long blue veins had popped out, entwining, and now rolling and pitching as he walked, as he shifted in his tall stool, as he watched, as if to recall the fight between his insides and his outsides. The muscles of his abdomen (I use the word like a professional, huh?) had slowly begun to tighten from this other temporal side, like a tapestry whose thread was being pulled, bit by bit by bit. He looked like he was working out! Samuel the body-builder, Samuel the catwalk model.

"Hey, you getting fit, Sam?" (a call from a bobbling fishing boat leaving the glittering harbor).

"*Pffffftttt!*" Samuel dismissive.

He was, despite things, aging gracefully from the inside out, particularly given the short time he had had to embrace the idea of being three times his age, that is. And yet, he was also aging with contempt for aging, not for the appearance of age but for the very idea of it. This is hardly a riddle. On the outer of him, nothing had changed. To use the well-known terms: he, you see, was not the dotard. He was not the veteran. He was not the fogey, the codger, the old kook. He later told me:

"Do you know, sometimes I could see my skin hanging over my elbows, even though it wasn't? Weird, yes?"

Weird. When Kitty Felmore asked him one day, on entering the offices: "Are you in a state of contemplation?" He heard instead:

"Are you in a state of dereliction?"

His exterior was growing displeased with his interior, so that had I not appeared when I did—brandishing a fine new filigree bat net and my best binoculars, if I recall, and as dusty as a cavalry mule—he might well have disappeared into his own fundament, in pursuit of final victory.

"Are you listening?" he shouted at himself, in the early evening offices.

(Sometimes when the cleaners were still there they scurried away, replying: "Yes, yes.").

"I win!" he shouted. And to make this irrefutable he took pains to forget everything he knew about the past and only to refer to the present and to the future. Some of the Communion Islanders visiting the Offices, often being the last surviving remnants of families whose histories were mixed in the stumbling medical history of those very islands, yet full and feisty with island pride, took offence at his immediacy and said things like:

"If you don't know . . ." and:

"If you don't remember. . ."

To which he replied: "You're doing enough remembering for all of us!"

When finally he announced his illness to the population he did so with the news that he had no intention of standing down from his position. He did the announcement as Communions fishermen and timbercutters and bird catchers and sailors and banana farmers and hostel operators came into the Offices one morning. He said:

"Just because I don't look that old doesn't mean I'm not."

When the audience naturally thought he was talking about his maturity and making one of those statements the immature make, he let the cat out of the bag. By which I mean he let fly his frustrations, he. . . Well, he filled that front room:

"Dying, probably," he shouted. And:

"How would you know?"

I think if we were in love before this (even though we had not yet met) we became even more in love during those moments. His voice was like a rushing flood from nearby the river, if that doesn't overstate the case, which wound up through the town and though at first that river is clear and blue and burbling bright soon, behind the old hostels and the shipyards and the fishmongers and the stonemasons and the oily yards where trucks were jigged up on blocks and stumps and men in overalls discussed grave mechanical consequences. When it reached up there, behind the town but not yet into the mountains, beyond the main stream and no longer navigable, then the Panapoon River grew dark and dirty and the mountains with their tar trees and blackwoods and the town with its people and its history swirled on together. And that was Samuel's voice at that moment, that was his father in the mountains and his grandfather like him and Samuel's restlessness and life and death.

"I'll be here," he continued, the thought of that morning's ghorbbi no doubt there on his mind.

(It is on mine now as I recall this moment).

Expectedly, however, much as he had risen up and filled that room more than one tenor, no matter how famous he might be, might ever have done his ageing inside rose up, or fell down (more accurately) with him at the same time, and he then slumped back behind the crowded desk as the mornings visitors then made their way into the building. Though I was not yet there, and cannot report more, I imagine as they wandered past, reading the sign that pointed them to Fisheries, or Agriculture, to Clerk of Works or to the Magistrate, to the small (and I can report not unattractive) little wooden alcove where Communion Islanders reported births, deaths and, also, marriages, that those islanders were full up with thoughts about the past and about the future, embodied as that was there in my young-old Samuel and slumped there as it was, awaiting the arrival of the island's new doctor, and hidden a little as it was from view behind the desk as Samuel, unwittingly, had now fallen to sleep.

DE PARTV, ET PARTVRI-
entium infantiumque omnifa-
ria cura.

CAPVT I.

Figure 24.

What a Women Looks Like When She Finally Turns Up

There I was, arrived. A pious hooded monkette, about to go trading leather bibles with confused natives, hanging on to the top of the big wooden door, my bag at my feet and my binoculars around my neck.

I guess you could say I was a fish out of water, flipping there in the Offices, whipping my tail there in the shallows.

Some madman in a seaplane had brought me down from the Cuuk (almost hitting the Akerondite mountains or some such, on the way. That *goof!*). I was filthy and hungry and thought I might have been coming down with some feverish ailment, one of those sub-tropical *olioila* viruses more than likely, I thought, or a case of blind panic. I had nothing but pictures of a return to drizzling dungeoned London in my head, the dread of the problems that would almost certainly entail and the sense that, were I right, and my application to The Communion Islands had been rejected, then there was nothing for it but to retreat into caves above the valleys of Cuuk, grow a bushy black beard, if an ordinary woman might have the ambition to do that, and live with the mighty *Macroglossus sobrinus*, the long-tongued fruit bat, whose colonies, I'd noticed, were tolerant of strangers.

The door on which I was hanging was one of those deep green ones with the frosted glass panels in lively bubbles and the sculptured lattice work and the glossy smooth paint. You know the kind. You can see these doors everywhere, in stories about small towns and train stations and school houses. I celebrate these doors. They are the doors to opportunity.

Although I'd been knocking on the door for some time, nothing had happened; and, exhausted, I had it mind to take to my bed (though at that point I didn't have one) and hope that in the midst of a deep sleep and a shot of Black Stag, which sat in a dark bottle in my overnight pack, that a solution to my predicament might stand up and, grinning at me with all its might, take me forth into the future without a whim or a worry. If I have an ability, a doctorly-trait, then it is to be crowned by enthusiasm and posed by joy, and in that enthusiastic regalness to find an optimism that bears little resemblance to the world we daily encounter. I am a partisan, a buff, a devotee. Needless to say, I am not a woman to begin work late or to treat effort with the laxity of those physicians who step into their consulting rooms at the hour, only at the hour, and depart by the hour for golf or sherry or the like. I am an enthusiast, a companion, a leader, an accomplice.

I thumped there on that otherwise positive green door. With the side of my filthy fist. My hand was getting numb. I thought a door in the rear might open and an old "guy" in a grey coat would come out, licking his fingers, and apologizing for having been consuming his soup. Though the door was ajar, and I could see in, I thought for a moment that I was mistaken and perhaps I was on the other side of an opaque boundary and what was in front of me—the shiny floor, the coco palm wood counter, the picture of the Bay of Shoals with its leaping dolphins and basking sea lions, the potted fig, the red plaster clock—was a kind of blurred mirage, and behind it was the real world, mechanical and brown. I had been traveling some time, and was tired, and what with the terror of return to my old life, the smell of coco plums, the speckled light through the frosted glass, the image of mountains looming suddenly through low cloud.

The man behind the desk emerged in stages. One, as he rose to desk height. Then two, as he rose further. Then three, as he leant (or slumped slightly, more accurately) forward onto the desk top. He scratched at his forehead. I saw that as he did so, methodically, intentionally, he seemed to be gathering up something (had I known his old self and his young self were battling I'd have thrown in a stick, or launched a length of pipe). *Scratch, scratch, scratch.* His fingers were raising little red tracks as he did this. It gave him the appearance of a tiger (or so I now remember; but that might be a vision brought about by my familiarity and love). He blinked at the speckled sun. He had a not unpleasant aroma of brine and undergrowth (possibly from having been on the not so scrubbed floor). There was an inquisitiveness about him and, if not to put too fine a point on it, a slight sense of the prize-fighter's viewpoint. I'd not always been around opera, around singers and marble staircases and hanging lights, tenors and their tenuous ways: I knew that fighter's world—the leathery thud of determination, the muscled miracle of recovery, the bloodied face of surprise.

I thought: "I had better give him a moment to compose himself, this man, this god." (though perhaps I add that now, the latter, after the fact).

Country boy that he was, Samuel then spoke up:

"It's alright, madam. I was only dreaming."

This statement he delivered to a spot above my exposed left ear. As we were already in love, and becoming more in love (well, this is how I see it), it is probably superfluous to say that I found at that point my desire to reach forward and cusp his jutting jaw almost insurmountable. I clutched at the green frosted anchor in my grubby left hand.

His voice crackled and shot. I thought of it, do you know, as fireworks? He danced (some might say that he swayed, but what do they know?). He seemed to gather up some energy from the air around him and, given the steamy scent of the offices I could admire the effort (I imagined this was like electricity raised on the static of wild perspiration and the shuffle of unknown sidereal time). Of course, you might be wondering where Penny Apple was located, as she was missing.

I like to imagine, in my quieter moments, when waiting stealthily in a tumble tree beside a damp cave entrance, or lying beneath leaves on a forest floor as above me begin to roost the shy *Acerodon jubatus,* the Giant Golden Crowned Fruit-Bat, whose hairy yellow plumes are prized in some cultures, that she was out on an oyster boat in a pair of khaki waders shucking spiny-backs into a bright orange bucket; or that she was climbing a tree on the nearest nut plantation, in search of the elusive macadamia. In fact, she was out at her grandmother's house helping with the chickens. *Cluck cluck clucking* about, with her hands in her apron, and seed flying hither and thither. You never can predict these things.

"Dreaming?" I asked, in a friendly fashion.

Later he would recall for me how he was feeling departure and arrival simultaneously, an impossible sense of being torn, torn that is into two creatures when, in fact, he was sure it was necessary for him to be one.

At the time his jaw dropped, and for a while no words came out at all. Then he said, as if he'd seen in me something that he had never seen before and spying this thing—what was it, my glittering green eyes, my heart-shaped lips, the cut of my jib around my greasy blouse collar and the scoop of my enormous shoulder blades (if I have any of these things)?—something I swear was:

"Pain."

"Pain," I asked. "Just now."

He was leaning forward onto his desk and staring at me.

"Washing through," he said.

"Oh," I replied. I wondered for a moment if I should have stayed in the air and perhaps have instructed the mad sea pilot to head due West until the tiny bucking seaplane ran out of its fuel and we plummeted, whistling, finally into the dark sea, relieved at least of the uncertainty.

"Do you fish?" he asked.

Something from his dream, I thought. I did not know, of course, that he had been out with his line that morning and what he was asking was a recollection rather than a fantasy.

"Not for fish," I replied, chancing some mild banter.

If I was to suggest anything I would say that at that point he was watching, somewhere over my head, a pelican flapping its gigantic pelicanesque wings as it cast its shadow over the vast ocean where, just beyond in their flighty way, skites skited and skimmed and nipped at the sea, drawing up from those deep, dark waters tiny gullets of flippering greenfish, which later these skiting skites would regurgitate onto the sands flats for their offspring.

"Well," he said, "I hope . . ." and his voice trailed off.

"Like a thief in the night," I laughed, winking a tired and filthy eye.

"Oh no!" he replied, "not like that at all."

I clawed at the air where I thought there was a swarm of tiny flies arriving and whizzing around my face; but, it turned out it was merely the speckling from the frosted glass and the air was perfectly clear.

"No, no," he said, seeming to come more awake.

His smile reminded me of silver and turquoise, for some reason, set in a deep rose gold.

"You have a fine place here," I said, referring to the Islands that I barely knew, but sensed I might be coming to know and to love. He looked around the room at its wood and polish, its windows and walls, its light fitting in brass and dim yellow light, handing low over the center.

And then I reached, and I took his hand. I took his hand as I would the hand of a famous singer, or a resident specialist, of a young and rising athlete or an old and successful gold prospector.

Figure 25.

A New Doctor in a New Town

I did not set out to impersonate the new island doctor, Thompson. Not him, the incoming Communions Islands' physician, nor any other. I had not spent my short time imprisoned in the Far East, awake at night, listening to those Eastern zithers and the Chinese lutes and inventing new identities for myself, of which The Communion Islands physician was the dominant and now prominent one. I had been far too preoccupied with other things: the amorous nature of the guards for one thing, who seemed to find in my bold mature spirit and attention to their minor medical ailments (itchy trigger fingers, bruised toes, slashed arms, and the like) some female solidarity, and were subsequently inclined to want to take that to its full and, as they saw it, logical end.

But I had not been there seeking change, only change of circumstance. And when finally I secured my most enduring medical appointment, as a personal medical assistant to a famous but unscrupulous tenor (whose medical conditions consisted mostly of "middle C throat" and "*leggero* tongue", with a touch of his persistent gout and the not infrequent hangover) I had not then sought out a new identity but thought my own was becoming more determined and bright.

Difficult employment conditions aside (a tenor is no pushover when it comes to habits of eating and sleeping, and one with a penchant for long nights at the Old Singapore Club and richly sauced game hens is inclined to struggle further to perform) I was proud and pleased with my progress, except in the small matter of continuing in my current post. The paradox, you might say, of a kind mind and kinder deposition. But I did not seek out to deceive anyone. I was not filled with theories about representation and belief. I did not think that if I shook a clerk's hand and said, brightly, "Hello." that I would become a candidate for a prime position in islands' medicine, or in law or politics for that matter—both of which have at various times intrigued me, if only because of their tendency to address the condition of humans and, simultaneously, the humans whose conditions they are addressing. I did not have thoughts, one way or the other, about the adopting of a medical persona where practice was one component and officialdom the other.

Undoubtedly, having studied the medical careers of the famous Rogers and Thibault, Champion, and Fu I had seen how a physician could step forth and embrace the wider purpose, take hold of it from behind and run forward with it in her firm arms so that as her career advanced so did her influence on society, one sprinting step at a time until, some time later, a long time later, staggering into her final and puffy years she would be awarded the Medal of Valor and the Prix du Nu and the Triumph of Medicine and, lauded by local and national dignitaries alike, on the Board of several Associations and Committees and Authorities, she succumbs to the physicians' version of exhaustion and a nasty skin complaint, and retreats finally into death.

But I had not arrived to impersonate, only to enquire.

Yes, my occupation was physician, and my interest was in the influence of the habitual consumption and behaviors of *Pteropodidae* and its several hundred lively and progressive sub-species on the longevity of certain patients, given my long term research on the matter and the results that appeared to be pertaining, or might be pertaining. Who knew? Thus was my ongoing research. Were they? Was it? Could it? Might it?

"Welcome," Samuel said, his briny hand in mine.

Automatically (if that is not a rude word) I thanked him.

"Come in," he said, with veneration.

"My clothes," he said, surveying himself. And as if I had come out of the dream he had been having, he began to apologize for his appearance—those grey shorts, that ragged orange toweling shirt - and to project me forward, only into the room, of course; but it was as if he was centering me beneath a much larger and much brighter light, the kind that contains monarchs, and adventurers and tropical homes with red canaries in bamboo cages and a resident crusty botanist who has discovered that the flower of the purple ylang ylang vine cures insanity, if only in those who are brought to it by circumstance not cognition.

Dear little bird, I thought, can't you see that I am as genuine as the day and as committed to possibility as a dawn?

"Sweet," I wanted to say, "look at me! I am tired and yet excited. I am in need of a bath; yet, strangely, feeling cleaner than I have for some time. You've already brought something out in me. You may know the *Cynopterus brachyotis* that is said to be a lesser bat and shorter of nose. But do you also know that it is the highest of all the bat fliers? Jet pilots have reported seeing them. Seriously! Experienced pilots, above thirty thousand feet. All these *Cynopterus brachyotis* swooping and diving and mating up there. I can but imagine!"

"Sweet," I wanted to say, "forgive me! I am not the woman you think I am. But maybe I am a better one, huh?"

But the way he was looking at me, the way he was leading me to the center of the room, the sound of sweepers whistling and whooshing on the street outside, the clanking of rigging over at the harbor, the bustling voices of the rough and ready hostels, the speckle of sunlight through the green painted door."

"Sweet," my head wanted me to say, "I am only a physician, and still quite a young one at that. At the moment I am trapped in Act Two".

But my heart had other plans.

"It's almost Arcadia here," I said, sweeping a theatrical look around the room, spying the final exit of that previous beetle, as it found a crack in the floor and tipping its beetling hat in my direction, and waving a spiny leg, slipped on into it.

I was still telling myself: "When he's calmer, I'll set the record straight." But my head and my heart were not in agreement.

I said to myself: "Despite his youth he seems strangely aged, matured like a length of wood that has been cut and stained and left in the sun."

Also: "He maintains youthful ways but he is not youthful really at all."

In addition: "He is more like a walnut, actually, with the outside green and hairy and the inside hard and shriveled."

My nutty lover. How much of this have I invented, after the fact, I wonder?

When he reintroduced me to Kitty Felmore, whose stingray hatted vista I had already encountered when landing at the tiny airport in that tiny plane in a tiny mess with a tiny intention of staying as tiny a time as possible and demanding an explanation of why I had not been contacted about the advertised post (Fate made no demand necessary, as it turned out), the shock on her face was almost enough to make me spit out the truth. But before I could do my spitting, Trevor, Kitty's short but heavy collared husband, stepped forward and, adopting the persona of a post office licensee, delivered me like a newly arrived package into the waiting hands of the room. His own hand—his right one, anyway—knew no restraint and he shook my own filthy palm with such vigor and force that had I truly been a glass vase sent by your Aunt Ethel, wrapped and taped in old newspapers and contained in a cardboard box, I'd have shattered apart and, falling out between your aunt's shaking tapings, ended up like so much sharp confetti on the floor of the room.

"Dear, dear, dear, dear," delivered Trevor, who I now know takes a bicycle spin just after dark, without lights, down the Skelton escarpment road, just after the post office is closed, facing death in order to keep him alive, and perhaps to put some spice into his days with Kitty.

'Dear, dear, dear, Doctor," he shook.

I told him to think nothing of it, though what he was thinking something of was entirely beyond me.

"I am sorry," rayed Kitty, as bright as a button and as round-faced as one too.

"Doctor," she said—this habit of address was forming quickly and I can't say it was upsetting me—"doctor, we almost sent you away."

I didn't recall any sending, but what the heck.

"I would have done the same," I said, "in my state". Thinking that any moment my appearance would give the game away and I was better to play that card than await my whole deck coming tumbling down.

She was right to suspect me, I said, playing things up.

I had come in search, but what I was in search of was no more defined than that, and if not for my exhaustion and the remnants of a flight on a small craft, down over territory I did not know and could not quite make out as the pilot pitched and yawed us up one valley and down the next, over a peak and under a hanging limb, and almost right into a cliff face. If not for that I might have been more on my game, more aware of the signals from behind Samuel's counter. Admittedly, in past years, I had worked at whatever was necessary.

A medical practitioner is no stranger to adaptation or the machinations of need, and I was no different to any other. In my pursuit of medicine I had husked wheat. I had hauled oysters from the briny lattices of their growth to the porcelain cups of their consumption. I had minded the pooches and pups of the wealthy and trimmed the beards of the bearded. When I was an intern, and earning no more a salary than a mountaineer earns the southern face of Kilimanjaro, I had mopped the floors of a train station, morning and night, seeing life pass before me on the way to somewhere, and on the way back, as I just moved back and forth between those four walls, going nowhere fast.

I was not a woman who had settled into one occupation in life and, privileged by money or fate or the depth of an inordinately inhuman intelligence, rose up through the ranks like a sapling that had found its rings one after another in quick maturity. A certain amount of inconsistency and uncertainty had always been my companion. I had not sought it out, but there it was and I was not one to ignore it, standing there on my shoulder with a twinkle in its eye and a tune on its lips. It had always given me something to which I might aspire, a flawed floor, on which I might build a better me. I was enthusiastic and effusive, and ready for anything.

Regardless of all that, medicine was my life and my comfort. It held a constant fascination for me. I believed, as an occupation and as a calling (as they call it) it suited my temperament, which has always been a tad toward the contemplative, and filled with the vision of something better. Call me a dreamer, or the descendant of one of those ancient telepathists who could see in the mist of an equally ancient lake or in their puddled reflection a picture of a new world and in that new world see themselves and their role and their future. When my future island patients came to me I felt entrusted with a great jewel, which was more than their lives but somehow the lives of all with whom they had associated - their lives too, and the licenses and sanctions they (often unthinkingly) had given out to others, and still others who had invested with or delegated to in knowing them. That was the extent of my telepathic feeling. I liked to watch those new patients enter and to imagine the great cavern of possibility illuminating as they slipped, apologetically, into the seat opposite me and to deposit the debris of unknowing out the window and reply as I asked:

"So what, today, is the problem?"

The problem, the potential, more like! Turning what was dirty and worn and unfounded into the empirical deity of truly magnificent modern human knowledge. What more could a woman want? We each have our place and I, in medicine and on The Communion Islands, had mine. My personality rose with it. My emotions too. I was known to fall into fits of tears at the sight of a child cured of a mere common cold. But what not?! Why not, indeed! What a miraculous foundation for all that is good. I was in no hurry to change all that, by taking on a role to which I was not suited. Nevertheless, there I was in the front room of The Communion Islands Government Offices, and there was Samuel, and there was a beetle making its brown tottering way across the polished floor, and there was an opportunity, and there was the speckled sunshine, and there was I, a simple animal, grunting "Yes, I have come to assist" when it would have taken no greater effort or attention to grunt: "Do you know directions to the beach."

It came as some surprise to me, sometime afterward when sitting above the vistas of Skelton Beach in the evening, with the twinkle of stars and the twinkle of huts on the twinkling beach below, staring down through the busy darkness, that it had been my voice that had been speaking. It could just as easily been the voice of some polar trekker who, having reached the ice drift on which a damaged steamer is, hoiks up my sealskin visor, pulls back my sea lion hat and, slapping the whale blubber greased on my chest and the charcoal on my hands, asks the huddled crewmen, there on their last legs:

"So, you have a little problem, huh? What can I do to assist?"

Vital Acknowledgments

To the faculty and staff of the Institute for the Medical Humanities at the University of Texas Medical Branch (UTMB), Galveston, with whom I spent time researching this novel as a Research Fellow in 2010. Thanks to the fabulous Dr Winslade! And to the fine Dr Brody! Thanks also to Drs Jones, Avery, Crowder, Clark, Hester, McKinney, Carson and more. What a fabulous, and fabulously generous, team! Thank you all.

Thanks also to Donna Vickers, Administrative Coordinator at Institute for Medical Humanities at the UTMB. Without you, Donna, nothing would have been possible. Warm thanks for your support and friendship.

To my colleagues at the Royal Society of Medicine (RSM), London, who not only maintain one of the best medical libraries in Europe, but also support a lively Fellowship, as well as the many physicians and other medical experts who do so much to improve human thriving around the world.

To Dr Robert Hicks, Sophie Sereda and Anna Dhody at the F.C. Wood Institute for the History of Medicine, the Historical Library and the Mütter Museum at the College of Physicians of Philadelphia. Thank you for a Wood Institute travel grant for 2012, and for your kindness while I worked in the excellent library collection there in Philadelphia.

To the US National Library of Medicine, "Images from the History of Medicine (IMH)" collection. Acknowledgment is made here of the location of these images and of the wonderful work undertaken by the National Library of Medicine, History of Medicine Division, in making them accessible.

To colleagues at Oakland University, Michigan - some of the finest folks you'll find anywhere.

To Dave Blakesley, a truly wonderful publisher, a founder who keeps on finding, or founding, if we happen to be making bells together, which might well be the case in some magnificent way! Here's to this and those beyond, Dave. You make the adventures happen! A magnificent creative and critical friend—it's been too long between drinks!

Finally, to Louise, and to our sons Myles and Tyler. This one has seen us on the road, in the air, and by the sea! In one house, and then another, on many different islands. With much much love, always.

About the Images

The author and publisher sincerely thank and acknowledge The National Library of Medicine (NLM), where these images are located. We believe each of these images to be in the public domain. If this is not the case we would be pleased to hear from any copyright owners who are not properly identified.

p. viii–Figure 1
Originally entitled: *Schema Instrumentorum Laboratorio Portatili Inservientium*
Becher, Johann Joachim, 1635-1682
Tripus hermeticus fatidicus, pandens oracula chymica, pl. 1
Images from the History of Medicine (NLM)

p.13–Figure 2
Originally entitled: *Operation for Removing Cataracts*
Bartisch, Georg, 1535-ca.1607
Dreszden: Matthes Stöckel], 1583.
Images from the History of Medicine (NLM)

p.20–Figure 3
Originally entitled: *Tweezers, Hooks and Other Instruments*
Vulpes, Benedetto
Napoli: 1847.
Images from the History of Medicine (NLM)

p.28–Figure 4
Originally entitled: *Instruments and Procedures for Head Surgery*
Armamentarium chirurgicum bipartitum, pl. 27, oppo. p. 38.
Images from the History of Medicine (NLM)

p.31–Figure 5
Originally entitled: Apparatus for the Tongue
Baratti, Antonio, 1724-1787, engraver.
Livourne: L'impreimerie de éditeurs, 17--
Images from the History of Medicine (NLM)

p.35–Figure 6. The Human Heart
Originally entitled: *The Heart*
Berengario da Carpi, Jacopo, ca. 1460-ca. 1530, author.
Isagogae breves, perlucide ac uberrime, in anatomiam humani cor-
    poris a communi medicorum academia .., l. 31 verso & 32 recto.
Images from the History of Medicine (NLM)

p.43–Figure 7
Originally entitled: *Figure Studies*
Images from the History of Medicine (NLM)

p.47–Figure 8
Originally entitled: *Ear Trumpets and a Clyster*
Bell, Benjamin, 1749-1806
A system of surgery, LXIV.
Worcester, Massachusetts: Isaiah Thomas, 1791
Images from the History of Medicine (NLM)

p.52–Figure 9. Woman Feeding an Infant
Originally entitled: *Ficta teneris immulget ubera labris*
Baldini, Filippo, b. 1750?
Metodo di allattare a mono i bambini.
Napoli: 1784.
Images from the History of Medicine (NLM)

p.61–Figure 10
Originally entitled: *Dies Microcosmicus Nox Microcosmica*
Fludd, Robert, 1574-1637
Utriusque cosmi majoris scilicet et minoris metaphysica, physica
    atque technica historia, v. 2, p. 275.
Oppenhemii: Johan-Theodori de Bry,: 1617-1621.
Images from the History of Medicine (NLM)

p.67–Figure 11. Arriving
Originally entitled: *Anatomy of the human male*
Pietro, da Cortona, 1596-1669.
Romae : Impensis Fausti Amidei 1741
Images from the History of Medicine (NLM)

p.71–Figure 12. Me Holding One of the Hats Belonging to Death
Originally entitled: *D: Georg: Nösler. Berlinensis Marchicus,*
Noessler, Georgius 1591-1650
Images from the History of Medicine (NLM)

p.84–Lucky Figure 13
Originally entitled; *Organi Olfactus*
Casserio, Giulio, 1561?-1616
Francofurti: Nicolai Bassaei, 1610.
Pentaestheseion; hoc est, De quinque sensibus liber, Tab. VII, p. 123.
Images from the History of Medicine (NLM)

p.99–Figure 14. A Birthing Chair
Originally entitled: *Birthing chair*
Roeslin, Eucharius, d. 1526
Argentine: Martinus Flach junior, 1513
Der swangern Frauwen und Hebammen Rosegarten.
Images from the History of Medicine (NLM)

p.113–Figure 15
Originally entitled: *Forensic medicine: Criminal in chains before Justice*
1739.
Commentatio in constitutionem criminalem.
Images from the History of Medicine (NLM)

p.119–Figure 16
Originally entitled; *A love philtre from the painting by Edgar Bundy, R.I.*
Bundy, Edgar, artist. 1862-1922,
London: s.n., 1894
Images from the History of Medicine (NLM)

p.126–Figure 17
Originally entitled: _Urogenital system_
Mercurio, Girolamo, d. 1615, Author.
Venetia: Gio. Bat. Ciotti, 1601.
Images from the History of Medicine (NLM)

p.132–Figure 18
Bacon, Roger, 1214?-1294
London: Tho. Flesher and Edward Evets, 1683.
Cure of old age, and preservation of youth ..., title page.
Images from the History of Medicine (NLM)

p. 143–Figure 19
Originally entitled: _Anatomy of the heart_
Rokitansky, Karl, Freiherr von, 1804-1878
Wien: Braumuller, 1875.
Die Defecte der Scheidewande des Herzens; pathologisch-anatomi
  sche Abhandlung.
Images from the History of Medicine (NLM)

p.147–Figure 20
Originally entitled: _Iliacus internus_
Yeates, Nicholas, fl. 1680-1681, engraver.
In the Savoy [i.e. London] : Printed by Tho. Newcombe for the au-
  thor, 1681.
Images from the History of Medicine (NLM)

p.150–Figure 21
Originally entitled: _Medical Instruments & Apparatus: Sphygmomanom-
  eter_
1883.
Wiener Medizinesche Wochenschrift, v. 33, n. 22, p. 674.
Images from the History of Medicine (NLM)

p.156–Figure 22
Originally entitled: _Feeling_
Images from the History of Medicine (NLM)

p.160–Figure 23

Originally entitled: *"In aid of sufferers," by H.R.H. Princess Louise; W. Hollidge sc.*

Louise, Princess, Duchess of Argyll, artist. 1848-1939,

Hollidge, W, engraver.

London : William Little, 1870

Images from the History of Medicine (NLM)

p.168–Figure 24

Originally entitled: *De Partu, et Parturientium infantiumque omnifaria cura*

Rueff, Jakob, ca.1500-1558

Francoforti ad Moenum, : [Sigismundi Feyerabendi,] , 1580.

De conceptu et generatione hominis, l. 18 verso.

Images from the History of Medicine (NLM)

p.175–Figure 25

Originally entitled: *Eye surgery*

Jonas Arnold delineavit.

Armamentarium chirurgicum bipartitum, pl. 31, oppo. p. 59.

Images from the History of Medicine (NLM)

About the Author

Graeme Harper (writing as Brooke Biaz) is a fiction writer, scriptwriter and cultural critic. He is Editor-in-Chief of the international journal, *New Writing*. His awards include the National Book Council Award for New Fiction (Australia), among many others. A member of the Welsh Academi and a former Commonwealth Universities scholar in creative writing, he is a Fellow of such organizations as the Royal Society for the Arts and the Royal Society of Medicine. He has held professorships and honorary professorships at a number of universities in the USA, Britain and Australia, and was the inaugural chair of the Higher Education Committee at Britain's National Association of Writers in Education (NAWE). He is currently Dean of the Honors College at Oakland University, Michigan, USA. Among his other works are *Signs of Life: Cinema and Medicine*, with A. Moor, *Small Maps of the World* and *Moon Dance*.